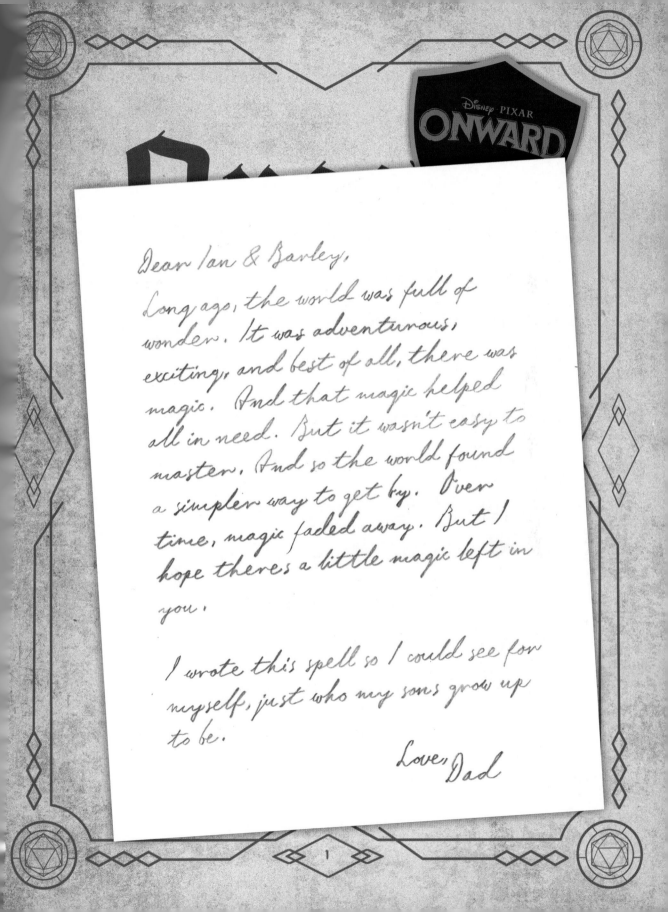

Dear Ian & Barley,

Long ago, the world was full of wonder. It was adventurous, exciting, and best of all, there was magic. And that magic helped all in need. But it wasn't easy to master. And so the world found a simpler way to get by. Over time, magic faded away. But I hope there's a little magic left in you.

I wrote this spell so I could see for myself, just who my sons grow up to be.

Love, Dad

Greetings!

In this tome, you shall learn of Quests and Magic, and become one of the brave heroes who seek to make the realm a better place.

You and your merry band of brothers, sisters, strangers, sages, and fools are about to embark on the epic . . .

Quests of Yore!

Within these pages, you shall find all you will need for a Successful Campaign:

Astounding Characters and Fearsome Beasts you will encounter—some will be friends; others will be foes.

Numerous **Spells** to master and hideous **Curses** to avoid!

The Fortitude to embark on a **Quest**, not for riches and glory, but for the improvement of the realm.

Onward Ho! Let not the Shadow of the Sunset touch our backs before we have met our Journey's End!

This book and my knowledge are all we need to succeed. That's what I'm afraid of . . . . .

The sunset shall never catch us!
Before the day is done, we shall complete our quest and my brother, Sir Iandore of Lightfoot, shall return our long-lost father to our side!

So swear I, Sir Barley the Bold!

It's not a quest.
It's just a very strange errand.
And anyway, I don't know the first thing about this stuff.

Fear not, little brother!

For a Quest, one must carry a noble name like a golden crest upon thy tongue!

Look deep in your Mind's Eye—and in your Eye's Mind—and see what's written there! If you need some assistance, use the charts below to determine your Quest name:

Select Your Favorite Character or Creature	Add suffix to your first name
Elf	-dore
Centaur	-ish
Troll	-ington
Merfolk	-ley
Satyr	-ham
Cyclops	-ich
Goblin	-son
Sprite	-las
Gnome	-ton
Dragon	-shire
Unicorn	-thorn

Select Your Ideal Adventuring Item	Add Adjective to Your Name
Spell Book	the Majestic
Armor	the Stouthearted
Steed	the Sagacious
Staff	the Magnificent
Map	the Peaceful
Sword	the Supreme
Shield	the Fearless
Compass	the Serene

Select Your Favorite Season	Add Your Hometown to Your Name
Winter	of Widow's Peak
Spring	of Featherferdshire
Summer	of Bogsley on the Moor
Fall	of Round Hollow Flats

Be warned: knowing what lies ahead is considered a form of cheating!

But if you feel the need to find something specific, then avail yourself of the list below:

A List of What Lies Ahead

Quest Master

Astounding Characters and Fearsome Beasts

Discover the myriad characters that inhabit the Questing Realm. Their unique qualities may be the ultimate factors in determining a Quest's outcome. Choose wisely, for these characters can make or break a fellowship.

And be wary of the fearsome be~~asts~~ encounter on your journey. Thoug~~h~~ beautiful and majestic, all are pow~~erful~~ the realm.

Who is embarking on this quest for the ages, you may ask?

Let me introduce our players. . . .

SIR BARLEY OF AWESOMESHIRE

(aka Barley Lightfoot)

Beauty: +10
Brains: +14
Wits: How is that different from brains again?

Sir Barley is known throughout the kingdom of Awesomeshire for his bravery in battle and his stunning good looks. Plus, he can write the entire Troll alphabet upside down and backwards (to confuse enemies).

Elves

SIR IANDORE OF LIGHTFOOT

Next we have...

(aka Ian Lightfoot)

Brains: +50 AT LEAST!
Magic: +100 OR MORE!
Charisma: Uh... LOTS of untapped potential!

Sir Iandore had been unknown in the questing realm until he burst onto the scene with a stunning display of magical skill!

We're getting a little ahead of ourselves.
More on that later.

Ian Lightfoot

Just to set the record straight, I am:

☑ A sophomore at New Mushroomton High GO DRAGONS!

☑ Having a really weird sixteenth birthday More like a really

☑ Not a wizard YET! EPIC birthday

Yes, I seem to have a tiny spark of magical ability, but I do NOT know how to use it.

I mean, the results weren't exactly great. Nothing to write home about . . .

We are totally writing home (and everyone else) about our adventures.
We gotta leave home first, of course.
And speaking of home ⟶

There are other aspects of the Elven culture to discuss — how their pointed ears can hear an adversary's footfall over a league away! Many of the finest Wizards have

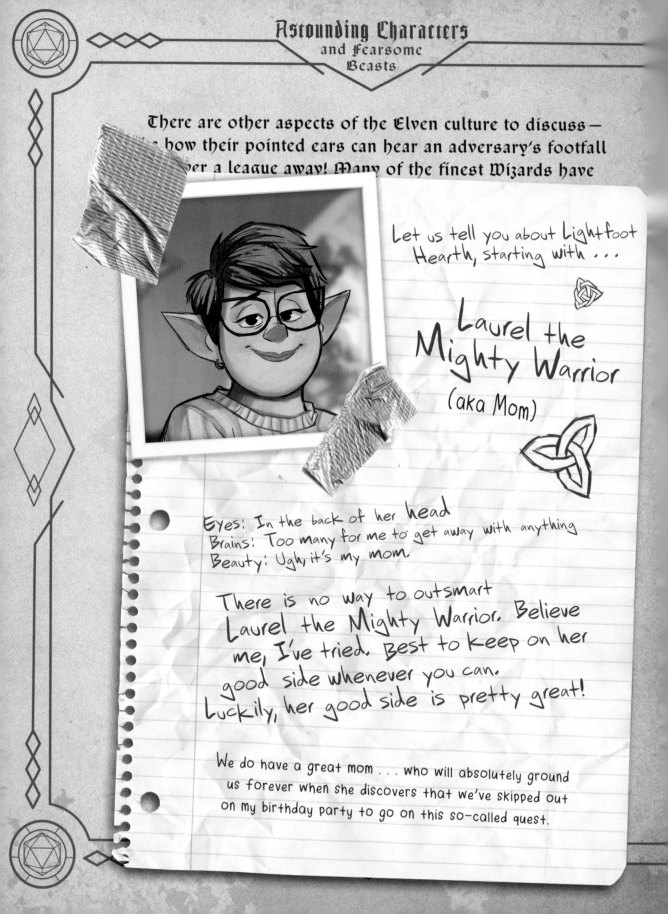

Let us tell you about Lightfoot Hearth, starting with . . .

Laurel the Mighty Warrior
(aka Mom)

Eyes: In the back of her head
Brains: Too many for me to get away with anything
Beauty: Ugh, it's my mom.

There is no way to outsmart Laurel the Mighty Warrior. Believe me, I've tried. Best to keep on her good side whenever you can. Luckily, her good side is pretty great!

We do have a great mom . . . who will absolutely ground us forever when she discovers that we've skipped out on my birthday party to go on this so-called quest.

Speaking of quests, ours revolves around this guy right here!

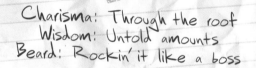

Wilden Lightfoot

(aka Dad)

Charisma: Through the roof
Wisdom: Untold amounts
Beard: Rockin' it like a boss

Wilden Lightfoot was known for his easy confidence and razor-sharp mind. Many moons ago, he vanished into the mists of time.

But this mighty wizard has recently made an EPIC return.

He's entrusted Sir Iandore and Sir Barley with a monumental quest the likes of which the realm has never seen!

It's kind of a weird story. It involves Dad's lower half.

How do we even begin to explain what happened?

Next we have... Officer Bronco, aka Officer Buzzkill aka Mom's boyfriend.

Colt isn't that bad. He's just very... I don't know...

Centaurs

Square?

It would be just our luck if found out about our quest. He never allows any horsing *around*

Really, Barley?

Maybe he should get his high horse. HA!

Wait! What was that?
There! There it goes again!
And yet again! Too fast for you to see!

You can bet your last bag of Goblin gold 'twas a **Centaur!** The fastest characters in all the realm, galloping at speeds of over seventy miles an hour. With their long, flowing manes, they are a wondrous sight to see. But do not be deceived by their beauty. 'Tis a mistake to get on the bad side (or the backside) of a Centaur. They are as quick to judge as they are to canter.

In addition, Centaurs are excellent hunters and trackers. Their endurance not only allows them to travel long ~~distances~~ ...s that they will remain ...wn any foe or goal.

Combat Expertise

Hunting and Tracking:
Can pursue and track down enemies

Stomping:
Uses hoofs to attack and defend

OFFICER COLT BRONCO PUTS HIS HOOF DOWN ON CRIME

New Mushroomton City Hall — In a festive ceremony this afternoon, Mayor Kingston awarded Officer Colt Bronco the "Citation for Bravery" in recognition of his successfully concluded investigation i...

What clouds of dust billow on the yonder plain?
Look closer! 'Tis a majestic Centaur galloping into the sunset!

THIS IS THE LAST TIME, BARLEY!

PARKING VIOLATION

Official City of New Mushroomton Notice: Improper Parking Citation

No. 149154

NOTICE
Vehicle is improperly parked. Violations are as follows:

- [ ] Expired Parking Meter # _____
- [X] OVER Curb
- [ ] Left Wheels to Curb
- [X] On a Sidewalk
- [ ] Blocking _____
- [ ] In a Fire Lane
- [ ] 15ft. of Fire Hydrant
- [ ] In Handicap Space

Date 4/27	Officer BRONCO
License No.	CUSTOM: GWNIVER
Make/Model VALOR	Color PURPLE/RUST
Location BURGER SHIRE	

TOTAL DUE: ___40___

All fines are 20 Shards unless noted. Fines are to be paid within 96 hours (4 days) of notice. After 96 hours, 20 Shard fines will be increased to 60 Shard fines. If fine is not paid within 30 days, a Citation will be given and said person will be subject to further fines and court costs for prosecution.

New Mushroomton City Hall
Elevensies Street
Suite 33
New Mushroomton, 157914
555-0101

FYI: Most cyclopes aren't amused by eye-related humor. Eye learned this the hard way.

Well, you can't always see eye to eye with a cyclops!

Cyclopes

Behold the All-Seeing Cyclopes!

Cyclopes may only have one eye, but with it, they see all the joy and folly this realm has to offer! They are clairvoyant and empathic—they can spot trouble coming from a mile away. This skill makes Cyclopes excellent team players, as they can see a dilemma from all sides and never miss the finer details.

Although Cyclopes excel as mediators, only a fool would attempt to deceive one. They can see straight through it! And when angered, they will track down an enemy in almost any terrain or condition. Their keen senses make them impossible to hide from.

◦ Combat Magnitude ◦

str	dex	con	wis
12	16	17	19
str	dex	con	wis
14	17	16	20
str	dex	con	wis
15	18	17	18

✝using 20-side die

A Cyclops warrior ready for battle

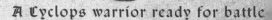

GO Dragons!

AUDITIONS

for the spring musical,

The Minotaur Cometh!

My kid made the
Honor Scroll
New Mushroomton high School

My kid made the Honor Scroll New Mushroomton high School

It's weird to see what everything was like back in the day. It's not really like that anymore here in the small town of New Mushroomton. I'll bet those ancient elves never had to deal with high school.

home

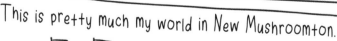

This is pretty much my world in New Mushroomton.

school

Trolls

Large heads! Large hands! Large appetites!
If one had to use a single word to describe Trolls, it
would be—HUGE!

Aye! A Quest does well to have a Troll among its
members!

They have no [...]
into battle with [...]
[...]ment's hesita[...]

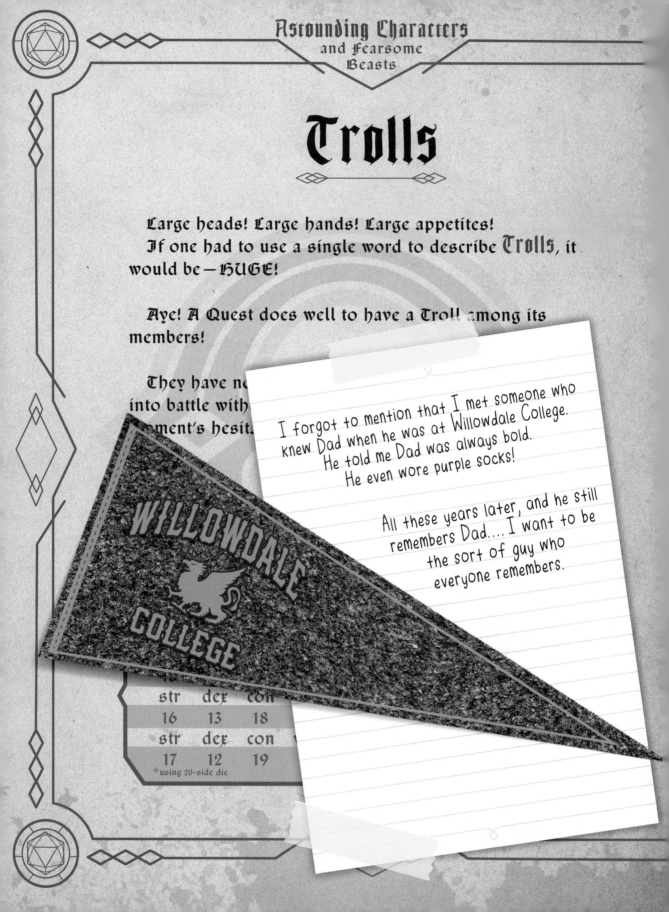

I forgot to mention that I met someone who
knew Dad when he was at Willowdale College.
He told me Dad was always bold.
He even wore purple socks!

All these years later, and he still
remembers Dad.... I want to be
the sort of guy who
everyone remembers.

str	dex	con
16	13	18
str	dex	con
17	12	19

†using 20-side die

Trolls may live under bridges, but they also build bridges of trust within their Quest clans. They are notoriously distrustful of strangers, particularly idlers, vagrants, and other suspicious characters who enter their territory. Clever and cunning, Trolls are skilled at riddles. They often require answers to their riddles in exchange for safe passage across their bridges.

Nowadays, you can just throw a few coins at them to cross the troll bridge. No one appreciates the secret art of the riddle anymore!

Ugh, traffic would be so bad if everyone still had to answer riddles.

Satyrs

Watch where you step! Do not trample that flower! Or strip that tree of its bark! Keep your senses keen. There are Satyrs about.

If your Quest should take you through the Woodlands, you will most likely encounter these Keepers of the Forest.

Satyrs (also known as Fauns) have a close connection to nature. They know how to read the stars and have a keen sense of direction. But do not mistake their love of nature for timidity—they are energetic and charismatic, which allows them to excel as dancers, musicians, and entertainers. They are also excellent jumpers who can leap several feet into the air.

Combat Magnitude

Die Must Match[*]

str	dex	con	wis
11	17	15	18
str	dex	con	wis
12	16	14	19
str	dex	con	wis
10	15	16	20

[*]using 20-side die

Their hooves make them resilient hikers, and their horns are a useful defense against any foes. Their head-butt alone can topple trees and shatter boulders.

But they are quick to anger if they feel you have transgressed their code of ethics. Indeed, they possess **Secret Knowledge**. You must charm them with fun and merriment if you wish them to share their **Wisdom**. . . .

NEW ME

- ☐ ~~Speak up more~~
- ☐ ~~Learn to drive~~
- ☐ ~~Invite people to party~~
- ☐ ~~BE LIKE DAD~~

I decided that my sixteenth year would be the start of the New Me. I'd be bolder and more confident. But everything went wrong.

I didn't speak up for myself when this guy had his gross feet on my chair.
I got scared during my driving lesson.
And I got all awkward when I tried to invite some kids over for my birthday party.

I wasn't able to accomplish anything from my list, but these latest events have given me some hope. Maybe, just maybe, all this crazy stuff can change things.

That's the spirit!
We are celebrating your day of birth with a solemn quest—
just like they did in ancient times.

Merfolk

Avast, young sailor! 'Tis not a pod of dolphins frolicking in the surf . . .

But a pod of Merfolk!

Merfolk (Mermaids and Mermen) are majestic as the deep sea itself, and have been said to breach from the water at immense heights. They can often be found racing swordfish or riding powerful ocean waves. Quick, agile, and resilient, they can brave the most dangerous of seas that no creature would dare sail upon. When it c...

Our dad was truly legendary.
Unfortunately, the details of the legend have gotten a little fuzzy over the years.

Here's what I remember about Dad:

1. His beard was scratchy.
2. He had a goofy laugh.
3. I used to play drums on his feet.

But with any luck, this may be our one and only chance to make new memories with Dad.

and Fearsome
Beasts

Goblins

Rough. Tough. Gruff. **Goblins.**

Almost like a poem, those four words. But there is nothing poetic about Goblins—either in appearance or attitude. They laugh rudely at the idea of "personal hygiene." They are happy to accompany you on a Quest, but beware: they have been known to double-cross their allies when it comes to riches, fame, and fortune.

Also be wary of trading with a Goblin, for they are tricksters. For this reason, Goblins often make the most successful and cunning of Rogues. With their cleverness and dexterity, they can sneak into and out of even the most heavily guarded dungeons, vaults, and chambers.

Combat Magnitude

Die Must Match[+]

str	dex	con	wis
13	19	15	17
str	dex	con	wis
11	20	13	16
str	dex	con	wis
10	17	11	15

[+]using 20-side die

Exchange or sell your goods at the local

PAWN SHOP

The Best Prices! The Squarest Deals!

Haven't Quested in Years?

Say Goodbye to that Dull Sword and Hello to a New Blender!

Turn Your Rusty Old Battle-Ax in for a Gently Used Lawnmower!

Our Trades Won't Be Beat. And You Won't Be Disappointed!

I got some awesome old swords for my collection here. I've had my eye on this one goblin helmet forever.

*"Used," "New," and "Disappointed" are terms open to interpretation and are not legally binding.

WHY WOULD YOU NEED A SWORD?

Ooh!
Cool band name. # Sprites

Are **Sprites** allies or enemies? Are they trustworthy or sly? The answer is a resounding **YES!**

There are many subspecies of these characters. Some are as shy as a newborn Satyr, others as crafty as a roguish Goblin. But regardless of their motives, Sprites are known to be friendly and whimsical. They enjoy good conversations and meeting jovial characters of all kinds.

They are also nimble fliers. They can travel long distances through any sort of climate despite their thin, ~~diaphanous wings.~~

They can't be that bad ...they're sprites!

HIGHWAY TERRORIZED BY SPRITE MOTORCYCLE CLUB

highway 3— A motorcycle club known as the Pixie Dusters is reportedly terrorizing commuters on the local interstate, but authorities are unable to find the alleged perpetrators. Several witnesses insist that the motorcycles are driving themselves. Officials are

Gnomes

'Tis another world below the Questing Realm! A world full of tunnels and treasure!

A world full of Gnomes!

underground as much anymore.

I don't think they live

Look at this flyer they left on our do

Be not alarmed! The Gnomes are a proud but shy and peaceful group and do their best to stay out of Surface Dwellers' way.

...rface

...pplies

...ve

...as ever

...t 'tis said

**SIGN UP TODAY WITH
THERE'S NO PLACE
LIKE GNOME—**
YOUR LOCAL PROFESSIONAL
GARDENING SERVICE!

WE ARE EXPERTS IN
Trimming
Planting
Tree Care
Dancing Cute Little Jigs

PAYMENT IS DUE THE FIFTH OF EACH MONTH.

WELCOME,
NEW CUSTOMERS!

e these the same trees who greet
you in front of Journey Mart?

Whispering Elms

One and the same!
they always know about the Specials and Sales.

You shall require a good compass and a keen mind if you venture into the Forest of **Whispering Elms**. While able to speak, move their branches, and shake their leaves, these trees cannot travel; they remain where they took root.

The Whispering Elms have all manner of knowledge that they have attained over their long lives. But beware! As their name indicates, they will listen in and whisper about any Traveler who should pass by. Not much can escape their watchful gazes. They do not mind visitors within their forests, but you must not overstay your welcome. Otherwise, the trees entwine the unworthy trespasser in their unyielding branches and hurl them as far as a kilometer!

Combat Magnitude

str	dex	con	wis
11	12	8	16

str	dex	con	wis
13	11	5	18

str	dex	con	wis
14	7	4	20

‡using 20-side die

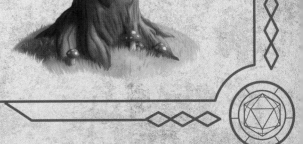

Griffins

We gotta g̶ to this plac̶

Now 'tis time to explore the amazing and fearsome Beasts that you may encounter on your journey, starting with the Kings of Beasts, the Rulers of the Skies: Griffins.

Gaze upon the Griffin in all its majesty. With talons as sharp as knives and wings that can swoop and soar across the skies, the Griffin combines strength, agility, and grace.

Numerous tales have been told of the Griffin's power, as they protect the realm from above. But they are known as fierce adversaries on the ground, hiding in t̶̶̶ unsuspecting pr̶̶̶

I could go for a griffin burger right about now. We need rations for our journey!

⸺ Combat Mag̶

Die Must M̶		
str	dex	co̶
9	13	4̶
str	dex	co̶
10	11	5̶
str	dex	co̶
8	14	2̶

✝using 20-side die

West Gateway County
Phoenix Farm

- Bring the kids to feed our flock of friendly Phoenixes!
- New Phoenix chicks to pet.

* 500-YEAR-OLD BIRDS KEPT SEPARATE IN CASE OF SPONTANEOUS COMBUSTION

DON'T WORRY! --> PHOENIX FIRE MARSHALL IS ALWAYS ON HAND

Rising
the skies
Phoenix.

Many
Adventu
mystery
of this
come.

When they have lived a long the
they self-combust into glorious
dancing flames — then emerge
from their own glittering black ash.

Combat Magnitude

Die Must Match[+]

str	dex	con	wis
7	8	10	4
str	dex	con	wis
10	5	6	2
str	dex	con	wis
6	9	4	7

[+]using 20-side die

These creatures were once rare and majestic... and now we're overrun with this vermin!

Unicorns

Beautiful. Magical. Virtuous. Pure. 'Tis none but the noble **Unicorn.**

These gentle creatures instinctively know when one is pure of heart. It's a sensation they feel in their horns, which are valuable instruments in seeking truth. For the most part, they are solitary, peaceful, forest-dwelling creatures that sharpen their horns on the bark of trees. They will only attack when defending themselves.

These noble creatures have been eating of our garbage can for the last three mo~ And they eat their own vomit. Ugh

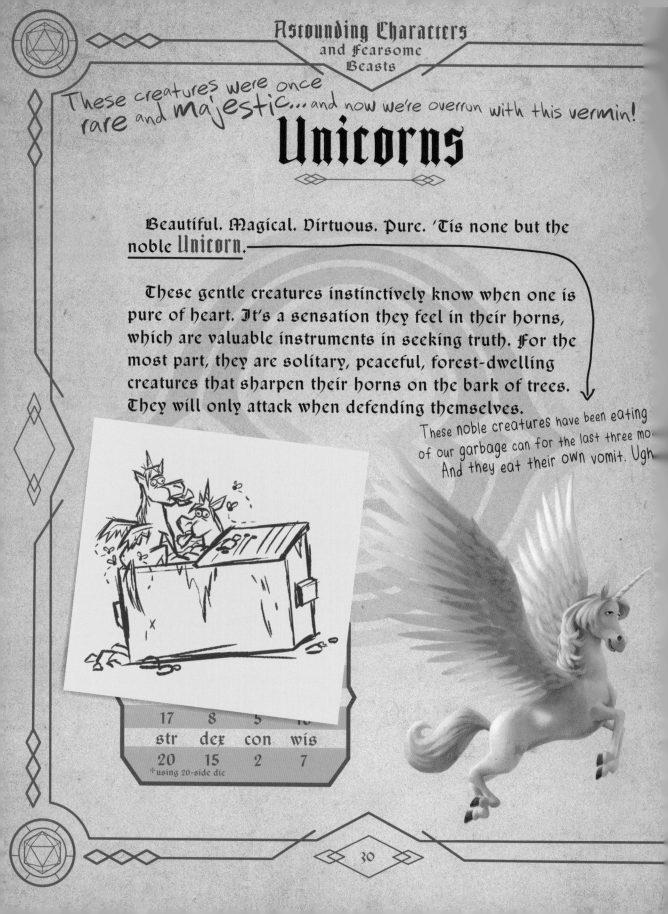

17	8	5	10
str	dex	con	wis
20	15	2	7

+using 20-side die

Speaking of noble creatures, I can't forget the most important player of this quest...

Guinevere

Faster than a **speeding state trooper!**
That explains all the speeding tickets.

Able to **leap** over a curb in a **single bound!**
Seems dangerous to go off-road driving in this....

Shining **headlights** when all other headlights have **gone** out! Well, <u>one</u> shining headlight.

Forget those garbage-diving rats with horns!
Guinevere embodies the true
SPIRIT of the PEGASUS!

I remember the first time I ever laid eyes on her.
I scoured for parts and put my heart and soul
into every last lug nut and brush of paint.
Guinevere is one of a kind.

Dragons

Even the bravest Adventurer will turneth tail and run when confronted by a Dragon.

And shrewd they are to do so! There are too many kinds of Dragons to remember. Some wise. Some wicked. But all have teeth to bite, talons to tear, and breath to burn!

Razor-sharp teeth

Combat Magnitude

Die Must Match[+]			
str	dex	con	wis
16	13	17	3
str	dex	con	wis
18	15	19	4
str	dex	con	wis
17	16	12	5

[+] using 20-side die

My little bro is a
wizard AND an artist.
LOVE IT! →

They are one of the greatest, largest, and thorniest
obstacles to overcome on a Quest.

Powerful wings

Long, whiplike tail

Thick talons

Foolishly approach a Dragon and, if you are lucky, you'll escape with your backside crisped to a golden brown.

If you shalt be unlucky, you'll end up in the Beast's furnace-like stomach. They are omnivorous. Which is a way of saying they will eat anything and everything!

But if one is brave (or perhaps desperate) enough to try to defeat such a foe, there are options. Average weapons will not be able to pierce the near-impenetrable hide of the Dragon. It is cunning rather than combat that will prevail in a Dragon battle. If one is looking to avoid a confrontation entirely, a Dragon Draught is often most effecting.

You don't know the half of Blazey has an appetite for socks, among many other thing

It's hard to believe that dragons were so ferocious back in the day

Believe it, little br

Everything in Quests of Yore is historically accurate!

I think Blazey could beat a hydra any day!

Hydras

Who's a fierce little monster?

Beware the many-headed **Hydra**.

This monster of the sea not only has its hulking size on its side, but it also has multiple heads that each have a mind of their own—and the ability to bite, tear, and thrash. Warriors have tried beheading the beast, only to discover that the heads grew back and multiplied—becoming fiercer and more terrible than before! Only the bravest and strongest of warriors (see the Manticore, page 71) can hope to defeat the Hydra. 'Tis best to escape as quickly as possible at the first sight of them.

Note: they have a penchant for sinking ships.

YOU ARE!

Combat Magnitude

Die Must Match†			
str	dex	con	wis
14	13	16	2
str	dex	con	wis
15	17	18	3
str	dex	con	wis
16	19	15	1

†using 20-side die

Giant Spiders

With numerous legs and even more eyes, Giant Spiders are some of the most treacherous creatures an Adventurer may encounter during their Quest.

Avoid dark and damp places where these Spiders roam, including caves, lairs, and wooded areas. Their webs are masterpieces in themselves, spanning many kilometers and displaying intricate details that are the envy of even the most skilled artists. But do not be fooled—these hypnotizing webs ensnare the Spiders' next victim.

That is disgusting.

Meh. Spiders aren't that bad.

But during one campaign my companion, Shrub Rosehammer, entered the Cave of Desolation and discovered an entire colony of these menaces! Even with his +10 agility and +9 cleverness, he couldn't escape the clutches of those ruthless arachnids.

◆ Combat Magnitude ◆

Die Must Match*			
str	dex	con	wis
16	14	12	2
str	dex	con	wis
13	15	14	2
str	dex	con	wis
12	16	13	3

*using 20-side die

Some say that this mysterious cube was formed in Hades's Kitchen from the bones of Baal himself.

Others say that the thickened blood of Oggendel the Twice Dead Troll formed its gelatinous exterior.

Those foolhardy enough to ~~meet~~ ~~make~~ this creature will discover a most unp_____ surprise. It is unstoppable. It is relentless. It is goo_____

Now THIS IS
TERRIFYING!!!
This thing CREEPS me out.
I never never never never never
never never never never never
never want to
run into one of them!
I don't really get it, but I'll take your word on that.

Notable Landmarks

Visit the wondrous, perilous, and impressive locations of the realm. From lawless taverns to mysterious caves, each place holds a wealth of wisdom and a variety of trials that are vital for all Adventurers to experience for themselves.

If you should remember only one thing, remember this: the direct path is not always the best path. Having faced no challenges along the way, the Adventurer on the clear route will be unprepared for the traps and tricks at the end of their journey. It is better to be buffeted by adversity from your very first steps. When you face the Ultimate Challenge, you will be battle-tested and emerge . . . Victorious!

Manticore's Tavern

7

Legendary Location

—— Level Seven ——

Start a new quest/fight an enemy. Roll for Danger & Luck.

So, we're finally about to set out on the quest.

I told Ian this is the first place we gotta go. All quests start here, and ours is no different!

First, let us start at the place where all Quests begin:

The Manticore's Tavern

Tall tales and clearheaded guidance will be found inside. But beware: this tavern is not for the faint of heart. It is full of miscreants and marauders who are as likely to empty your pockets as they are to disband your party. For the brave souls venturing forth, see page 71.

What are we waiting for?

Our chariot awaits!

The Fountain of Fortune

DISGRUNTLED CITIZEN STAGES PROTEST AT TOWN FOUNTAIN

Look! I'm famous!

This fountain should be a historical landmark. Great adventurers used to come and drink its cool, refreshing waters. Why won't people take me seriously?

Maybe because last week you claimed that the wall behind Burger Shire was also a landmark that deserved preservation and respect?

I thought I saw an ancient symbol engraved in the stones!

I hope my chant catches on!

New Mushroomton—

The dilapidated fountain in downtown New Mushroomton recently became the subject of a protest. The lone protestor chained himself to the fountain and, according to several eyewitnesses, could be heard chanting, "The days of quests were the best!"

The fountain, which has fallen into disrepair over the years, is soon to be torn down. "It's an eyesore. I don't know why he cares so much," said one onlooker. "I, personally, would rather see it be replaced by something useful, like a community garden."

The protestor was not available for comment.

Labyrinth

Woe to you, unlucky Adventurer, if your Quest leads you through the **Labyrinth**.

Many a Campaign has ended in ignoble defeat inside its confusing confines. For it taketh a clever, cunning mind to unravel the Riddle of the One True Route to Freedom. Legend tells of a terrifying Minotaur who lives inside.

A "terrifying Minotaur"?

Is that the mall cop who rides around and looks out for shoplifters?

One and the same!

Find A-Maze-ing Deals at the LABYRINTH MALL!

If only I could have seen this place in its prime! But it was either turn it into a shopping mall or see it demolished. It's really hard to find the food court or the shoe store or the bathroom ... or really anything, though.

The Path of Peril

It is unclear whether one is lucky or unlucky to discover the Path of Peril.

Spanning miles upon miles across the land, this route is not for the faint of heart. Adventurers can expect to encounter various terrains and obstacles, such as a forest of giant beanstalks reaching into the sky, towering mountain peaks, and treacherous cliffs.

The path ultimately leads to Raven's Point, the highest peak in the mountain range. Braving the Path of Peril is an essential milestone for anyone wishing to become an experienced Adventurer. The perseverance, courage, and wisdom to be gained from such a journey is worth more than any treasure.

Ooooh! The Path of Peril!
This is the stuff that questing dreams are made of!
This ancient road is iconic in the Questing Realm.

Barley, this is all very interesting, but why do
I need to know this stuff?

Patience is a virtue, my young sorcerer. We must be
prepared for ALL possibilities on our campaign.
And thou art an apprentice still. READ ON!

The Bottomless Pit

Not so fast, young fool! One slip of the boot and you shall plummet! And once you start falling, you will NEVER stop! Pray that you have brought a good book or a lively conversationalist with you—lest you go mad from the unending fall! Falling forever does not seem like a good way to go. Yeah, but the worst part of falling is landing! So we're good!

The Cave of Shadows

With this cave, there is more than meets the eye. See those symbols? 'Tis a puzzle for you to solve. Otherwise, prepare to be assailed and injured by all manner of weapon! But it's also the source of much Magical history, such as the mural below. Many a Wizard has ventured into its depths to obtain wisdom and clarity.

Objects to Be Brought

Now that you are ready to embark upon your Quest, here are some items that will be essential for your journey.

Sustenance — Food is of the utmost importance for a traveling Quest party. It will keep up your energy, and keep your focus off your stomach and on more important concerns. Hunting is not always possible, so bring hearty items.

Compass — Spend the extra gold and purchase a compass with Curse Guard. Otherwise, you might end up traveling in nonexistent directions.

Map — Sometimes it is best to let your feet wander where they will, but it would be silly getting lost in your own fiefdom before your Quest has really begun. A map will keep you on track no matter where your Quest may lead. Proceed to the Manticore's Tavern to obtain a map for your Quest.

Flask, Flagon, Cask, or Barrel — Depending on how large a thirst you work up on a typical Quest, you'll need something in which to carry your rehydrating liquids. Bringing a barrel can be inconvenient, but it also gives you something to bathe in when your smell groweth rank.

Weapon — Danger and peril are an inevitable part of the Quest experience. Indeed, many weapons have become legendary in the Questing Realm (see the Manticore's Curse Crusher or the Shield of Zadar). Be prepared to defend yourself against monsters or traps.

Wizard Staff — A sturdy staff can aid an injured Adventurer or keep a weary Traveler from slipping into a Bottomless Pit (see page 44). If thou hath the Magic Gift, then your staff can aid you in casting Spells and warding off Curses.

Non't need to shop for one of these.
We got an awesome staff
from our dad!
All we need for our Quest are the
things on MY list....

Sir Barley of Awesomeshire's Awesome List for Awesome Quests

<u>Refreshing Beverages</u> — Water is cool, but why not jazz things up a little and join the CARB-O-NATION?

My favorites:

Kobold Cola and Mountain Doom.

<u>Supreme Snacks</u> — Unlikely we'll encounter any wild game on Highway 3. And I'm not "game" to eat roadkill. Better to fuel up on cheese puffs, Sparkle Sticks, and griffin jerky. Could we get some real food?

<u>Epic Mix Tape</u> — The right music can keep a weary traveler from falling asleep at the wheel! NOT that I ever fall asleep at the wheel! Just talking hypothetically here.

A Mighty <u>Steed</u>- Unicorns are in no condition to ride these days. Fortunately, we have Guinevere. Who needs a horse when you have 150 horsepower?! HUH?

That's a very uni-corny pun.

<u>This Book</u> - Sure, I'm currently reading it and making notes, but what if I put it down and then forget to bring it?

partner

A Trusty ~~Sidekick~~ -
I would be nothing without my sidekick and brother, **Sir Iandore.**
Who would I gift with my encyclopedia-like questing knowledge?

A plan—that would be good to have on a quest, right? Following my gut is my plan!

Objects to Be Sought

Have you gathered everything you could possibly need for your Quest? Good. Now throw half of it away! Do not overburden yourself with bric-a-brac. There are far more important **Objects to Be Sought** as you go a'Questing.

Special Plants

Towering Toadstool — Not only provides shade and protection while exploring a forest, but its springy cap is an excellent launchpad to reach higher altitudes.

Gold Blossom — Discovering a flower with ten petals has been known to bring the finder good luck. But it must be in pristine condition and left alone — picking one will result in bad luck!

There are certain instruments that are imbued with Magical properties. You cannot know which have them without playing them. 'Tis good to have an Adventurer with musical ability among your number. *Does being great at air guitar count?*

Musical Instruments

The Lulling Lute — Will defuse a hostile situation. Dispels anger, disagreement, and general discontent. *Will not work on someone who is really just a jerk.*

The Fiddle of Fire — Is good for inspiring a dispirited group. Even the most charismatic leader will sometimes struggle to find the right words.

Great for public speaking!

The Harp of Harmony — Will make a mismatched group of Adventurers work well together. Once you have everyone cooperating, get someone to carry the Harp before the Spell wears off.

Enchanted Accessories

When entering a new village, be sure to check the market for **Charmed clothing**, **Bewitched jewelry**, and **Magical treasures**. Be warned! Such items are rare.

Giant Troll's Boots — Will make the wearer run thrice as fast as normal.

Goblin Cuff — Made of Goblin steel, this cuff gives the wearer fortitude and courage. It has also been known to increase one's strength for a limited amount of time.

Sprite's Lantern — Has the power to reverse Invisibility Spells and decipher messages that have been written in code. Be sure to give the Sprite a break from time to time.

I could use this because I can't figure out what Barley is talking about half the time.

The Dragon's Coin Purse — Will never be empty. No matter how many gold coins you pull out, there will always be more if you have noble intent. Take heed! The coins themselves have no intrinsic power. Spend them as you would any form of money.

Twenty-Sided Diamond — Forget about cut, color, clarity, and carats. The fifth C of diamonds — COUNT — is the only one that matters in the Questing Realm. Count the facets of a diamond, and if you come up with twenty, you may "count" yourself lucky! This diamond will increase the sparkle and power of Fireworks and Light Beam Spells when used with a Wizard's staff.

Dragon Teeth — Look for Dragon hatchlings' baby teeth in abandoned Dragon nests. One Dragon Tooth doubles the chance that Light, Wind, and Fire Spells will work. A whole set of teeth guarantees their success.

Aw, man! We should have kept Blazey's baby teeth.

We'd definitely have a whole set based on the number of times she's accidentally bitten us.

Elvish Emerald — This stone bestows Wisdom upon the holder. When used with a Wizard's staff, the stone will amplify emotion-based Spells such as the Calming Spell (see page 120) and the Truth Spell (see page 155).

I think we could use some of this wisdom right about now.

Unicorn Crystal — Shaped like the horned head of its namesake, this crystal will give potency to all animal-related Spells, like the Nature Speak Spell (see page 126).

Phoenix Gem — Among those most potent of Magical treasures, the Phoenix Gem amplifies the power and effectiveness of the most difficult Spells.

REMEMBER THIS FOR LATER, IAN!!

Curses to Avoid

Quests come with many hazards, but none are feared more than Curses.

Curses are Spells of misfortune that protect powerful Magical objects or significant locations. Some are more deadly than others, but all contain a core, the center of the Curse's power. Very few Adventurers have the abilities and the tools needed to destroy a curse. One such Adventurer is the Manticore and her legendary sword, the Curse Crusher (see page 72). But for most, Curses must be avoided at all costs, regardless of skill level.

If you should ever encounter a Curse, 'tis best to turn tail and run! But for your education, the following pages detail a few of the most common Curses, starting with the most dangerous one of all.

Curses?! You didn't say anything about curses!
Not to fear, young mage.
The likelihood of us encountering an ancient curse is pretty slim.
But we should always be on our guard!

What happened here?

Guar

known

I was trying out the good
ol' quill and ink like in the
days of yore, but the ink
kinda got everywhere.

I hope this page
wasn't important....

Fire Curse

The Fire Curse is among the wickedest of the known Curses, turning an element that warms a weary Traveler and lights their way into an Agent of Destruction.

The Fire Curse can take many forms.

Two of the most common are:

<u>Candelabra Conflagration</u> — Beware of candles that light too eagerly.

<u>Rain of Fire</u> — The most severe form of the Curse. Rain becomes flames that shower down upon the nearest village or dwelling.

Could be, but the beauty of the quest is discovering its secrets for ourselves!

Water Curse

Similar to the Fire Curse, the Water Curse transforms what is typically a beneficial element into something deadly. One must be extra cautious around aquatic Questing landmarks such as oceans, rivers, and lakes.

This Curse can appear in multiple forms:

<u>Dry Spell</u> — Can dry up bodies of water, leaving once lush land completely barren.

<u>Raging Rapids</u> — Even the calmest waters will become a torrent of crashing waves. Can also create whirlpools.

Weapons Curse

The Weapons Curse is a cruel Curse indeed! A weapon can be an Adventurer's ultimate protector when there are monsters about. And to haveth that protector turn on you? 'Tis enough to break the bravest Warrior's heart! May this list help you to avoid such a tragic end.

Savage Sword — The blade becomes dull and the handle suddenly sharp.

Cursed Crossbow — Don't shoot this cursed item, lest you want a boomeranging arrow speeding toward you.

Yowch!

Legendary Relics

You have, of course, heard the tales of the celebrated Adventurers of old! But did you know that many of the Legendary Relics from those stories have become just as famous as their keepers? Some are now owned by collectors and museums, while others have been lost in the mists of time. Perhaps YOU will be the fortunate Adventurer who discovers them. . . .

Bozark's Hammer — Was used to topple the Neverending Wall and unite the warring lands of East Westphalia and Northwest Southphalia.

The Hammer symbolizes the peace and prosperity that come when we find common ground.

This mighty weapon is on display at the Manticore's Tavern! That place is full of history. You're gonna love it, Ian!

Pretty sure I've seen construction workers use hammers like these.

This one is also with the Manticore!

Faldar's Horn — Saved the Peoples of the Accursed Archipelago from Gargamon the Dreaded Dragon. The Horn represents the importance of Vigilance in dangerous times.

Gargamon's Tail — Belonged to the aforementioned Gargamon the Dreaded Dragon. On the anniversary of the Dragon's defeat, the Peoples of the No-Longer-Accursed Archipelago would celebrate with a yearly carnival and parade the Tail around their capital city.

The Tail makes it clear that even the mightiest among us are destined to return to dust.

Boy, these guys really like to rub it in!

And I'm sure plenty of dust is gathering on the Tail, wherever it might be!

Chantar's Talon — Chantar, another Dragon of old, took pity on the nearby village of Skyehaven that suffered misfortune after misfortune. The benevolent beast gifted one of her talons to the villagers, and it is said that her Magic protected the village and brought endless prosperity.

The Shield of Zadar — Was used by its owner, the giant Cyclops Zadar, to stop the Torrential Tide from flooding the Thirteenth Colony of Desolation Island. The waters were diverted around the city and into an enormous hole in the middle of the island that Zadar had dug with the huge shield.

The children of the Colony still frolic in the waters of what is known as Zadar Lake.

Hey, Ian. Have you ever seen the Veil of Invisibility?

No . . .

No one has—it's invisible!

HA HA HA!

Hilarious.

The Tooth of Zadar — Was knocked from the mouth of Zadar the Cyclops when the Torrential Tide hit his shield. Grateful for Zadar's assistance, the city artisans of the Thirteenth Colony incorporated the Tooth into the Statue of Zadar that still stands on the bank of Zadar Lake.

I've been telling Mom that we should visit Zadar Lake for our next family vacation. It'll be educational AND fun!

I get that these things used to be important, but why do they matter now? They're just a lot of old things that belong in a museum somewhere.

Bite your tongue! All this magical knowledge can help us on our quest. You can't doubt magic when it brought our dad back to life!

ALMOST brought him back. PARTIALLY brought him back.

You got him locked in from the waist down. Just need the seeing and hearing part, and then we're gonna have a legendary family reunion!

Dad was such a bold and confident guy.
I wish some of that would rub off on me.

The (Bold) Apprentice

Adventurer, at this stage, you have discovered:

The Characters, Creatures, and Beasts you shall encounter.

The Lands you shall traverse.

Your Objects to be Brought and Sought.

The Curses you may face.

You are now prepared to begin your education in Magic. A fellowship would not be complete without a Wizard, so it is of the utmost importance that you pay special mind to these pages. Becoming a Bold Apprentice is merely the first step in a Wizard's development.

Any Wizard would declare that wielding Magic is all about the practice of Magic. One can only memorize Spells at home for so long. 'Tis vital to strike out on the trail and put thy knowledge into practice. If thou hath the (Magic Gift) nothing is more critical than actual experience out in the realm.

Oh, there is NO doubt that Sir Iandore has the magic gift.
We were all just sitting around about to start Ian's birthday party, when BAM-

Dad surprised us with the
MOST AWESOME GIFT EVER.

Mom gave me a gift that Dad wanted Barley and me to open after we were both sixteen. It had apparently been sitting in our dusty attic for years. There was a wizard's staff, a note with a spell, and a shiny orange gem!

A PHOENIX GEM!

I didn't even know Dad was into magic!
I'll admit, it was pretty awesome.

Point is: Dad was a WIZARD!

HOW COOL IS THAT?

Visitation Spell

 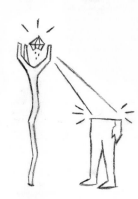 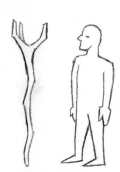

Only once is all we get
Grant me this rebirth
Till tomorrow's sun has set
One day to walk the Earth

This is the spell that came
with the **magic staff.**

I tried my best to get the spell to work. I read the spell over and over. But DESTINY HAD OTHER PLANS! Ian reads the spell ONE TIME, and the wind starts SWIRLING, and the magic staff and Phoenix Gem start SHOOTING out beams of light. Just like that, Sir Iandore brings our dad back with wizard-like ease!

I don't know if you could really call the spell a complete success. The magic was too strong, and it sort of ... backfired. It only brought back Dad's ... bottom half.

Dad may not be able to see or hear us (YET), but he knows we're here. I made sure to drum on his feet just like I did when I was little, and he responded to it with foot taps back to me!

The spell says we only have Dad for a day, so Barley thinks we should set out to find another Phoenix Gem and retry the spell.

Dragon ~~~~
Missing Gem. But ~~~~

☐ Play catch

☐ Take a walk

☐ Heart to heart

☐ Laugh together

☐ Driving lesson

☐ Share my life with him

Before we set out on our quest, we made a disguise for Dad. It may draw too much unwanted attention if we let him wander down the street as a pair of pants sans torso.

I also made a list of all the things I want to do with Dad when he's completely here.

I just hope we have enough time.

LET THE QUEST FINALLY COMMENCE!

I CAN'T WAIT!

If there is one name that you shall remember, let it be the most impressive, dreadful, inspiring, and terrifying of them all . . .

The Mighty Manticore!

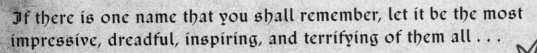

She can breathe fire!

The Manticore is both an intelligent creature and a brutish beast. With the mane and ferocity of a lion, the tail and sting of a scorpion, and the wings and temper of a bat, the Manticore is not one to be trifled with. Her claim to fame is punching a Hydra from the sky with a single hit. And she has a penchant for seeking out and battling any who attempt to bring destruction to the realm. To all the poor souls who encounter her: BEWARE.

But all Adventurers would be wise to begin their Quests at the Manticore's Tavern. 'Tis the place where all characters converge before setting out on their journeys. The Manticore herself is a deep source of knowledge when it comes to Quests and holds a collection of maps for various adventures. For anyone who is uncertain about their journey, one need only remember the Manticore's famous saying:

She is a LEGEND.

"You have to take risks in life to have an adventure."

I've never had the nerve to go up and talk to her.

Why do you insist she'll know where to find another Phoenix Gem?

I any remember: all quests start at the Manticore's Tavern. We NEED to see the Manticore so she can provide us with a map to the location of a new Phoenix Gem.

The Curse Crusher

There are many shields, swords, and axes of legend, but none is more legendary than the sword of the Manticore, which is almost as legendary as the Manticore herself. 'Twas forged with the rarest steel by Zobrak, illustrious grandfather of Bozark the Benevolent. It is forever known as the Curse Crusher, for its rare metal has the ability to annihilate even the most powerful of Curses.

How handy would this legendary sword be?!

The Manticore sounds kind of ... dangerous.
Are you sure she'll give us a warm welcome?

I'm not gonna lie, things are about to get HEAVY!
Ooh, this is gonna be good!

The Manticore's Tavern

This is the place where all Quests begin. Gather your map, your supplies, and your courage. And if you are a solitary traveler, you may create a fellowship here. Rogues, Warriors, Wizards, and characters of all sorts congregate here before setting off on their journeys.

When the Manticore is not out on a Quest, you will find her here, carousing and playing games of chance. At one time, the tavern was the Manticore's family home. She lived there alone for many years until one day, she decided to make it a place for Adventurers to come together and help each other on their noble Quests. She singlehandedly transformed her home into the most important landmark in the Questing Realm.

'Tis a place that most Adventurers would prefer to avoid. But there is essential knowledge to be gained among the No kidding! Reprobates and Rogues. So place your hands over your pockets, lest they be picked, and come forward! Your Quest begins inside. . . . Please no.

The Manticore's Tavern!
The place where all great quests begin!
Let's go! I hope you're right about all this. Just let me do the talking. She'll only respond if we show her proper respect.

TALON lickin' good!

> Life is an adventure...
> and so are our
> Spicy Kracken Kracklins!
> — "Corey" the Manticore

the Manticore

Warrior
Level Ten
Roll to summon mighty Manticore for assist in battle.

Wait, is this place legit?
I have a lot of questions.
Trust me.
Regardless of how the place looks,
the Manticore is the real deal.
There's more than meets the eye.
We'll find what we need here!

The Manticore's Tavern can be ~~overwhelming~~! _under_
But steady your heart!

Slow your breath!   _Trust me, I love the Manticore, but I hate what her tavern's become!_

Blend in as best you can amongst the Scoundrels!

Like the little kids at table 12?

You may need to behave quite badly to be accepted amongst their villainous lot.

But 'tis worth it to gain an audience with the Manticore.

Are we talking about ... the mascot?

When seeking favor with the Manticore, bow thy head.
Look at the ground. Declare thy unworthiness. Declare it
again! Remind her of her fearlessness, such as when she
vanquished the Hydra with a single punch. Or defeated
a den of Dragons with only a stone. Approach in this
manner, and perhaps the Manticore will show you favor.

Otherwise, she shall sting you with her scorpion tail and
roast you with her fire breath! Best of luck to you and your
fellowship in receiving the Manticore's wisdom. She will
provide the guidance you need for the successful launch of
your Quest!

We found the Manticore. It didn't go so well.
She didn't want to give us the map to the Phoenix Gem
because she was worried about something going wrong.

But in a surprising twist, Sir Iandore asserted himself!
He got up in the Manticore's face and
reminded her of her own saying:
"You have to take risks in life to have an adventure."

Dad inspired me to be bold... which then inspired
the Manticore to set fire to her own tavern.

We finally awakened the
true wild and dangerous
Manticore from her slumber!

Thanks, Kayla
We owe you one.

Hey kids! help me...,

FIND THE phoe ge

Unscramble
the letters
to tell
How to
FIND the
GEM!

ANERNOS

RAVENS P

Kayla
iX

Kid's menu

All entrees come with manna
fries, fruit cup & drink

Griffin Wings ----- $4.49
Medium or Fire Breathing

Kraken Legs ------- $5.49
With Brine Sauce

Roast Beast -------- $5.47
BBQ or Dry Rub

MannaChos -------- $4.47
with Griffin ----------- $5.47

Potions
Mt. Mist, Mt. Doom, Cloak
Root Ale, Dr. Fizzard

Faewild Tea & Water

P I T

INT

The Manticore said that it's based on the
real map. And it looks like little Kayla
already solved the puzzle for us. All we
have to do is go to Raven's Point!

The real map burned in the fire.
All we ended up with was
this lousy kid's menu.

Thanks, Kayla!
We owe you one.

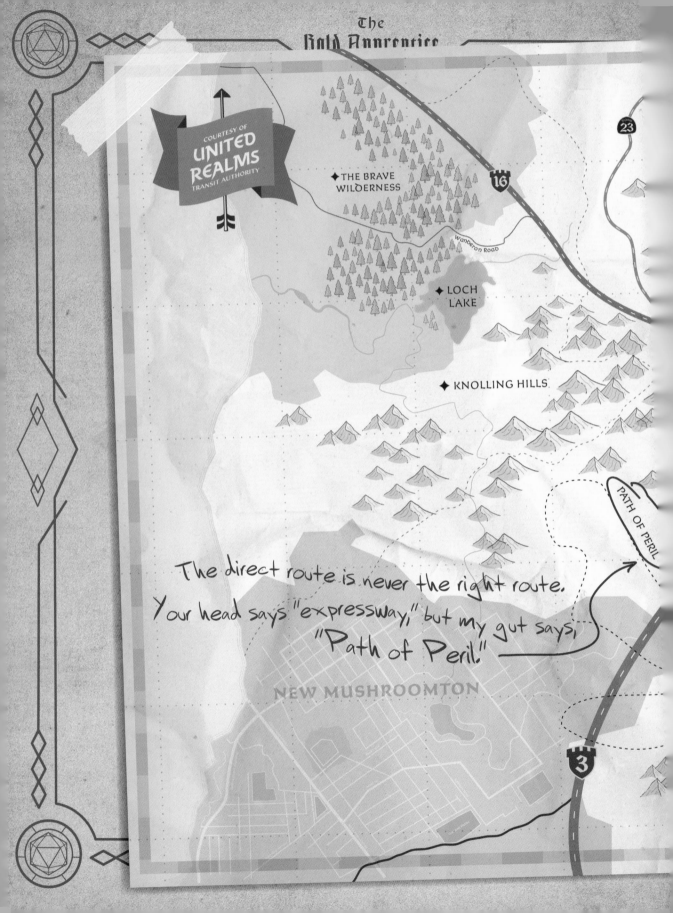

COURTESY OF
**UNITED
REALMS**
TRANSIT AUTHORITY

◆ THE BRAVE
WILDERNESS

Wanderon Road

16

23

◆ LOCH
LAKE

◆ KNOLLING HILLS

PATH OF PERIL

The direct route is never the right route.
Your head says "expressway," but my gut says,
"Path of Peril."

NEW MUSHROOMTON

3

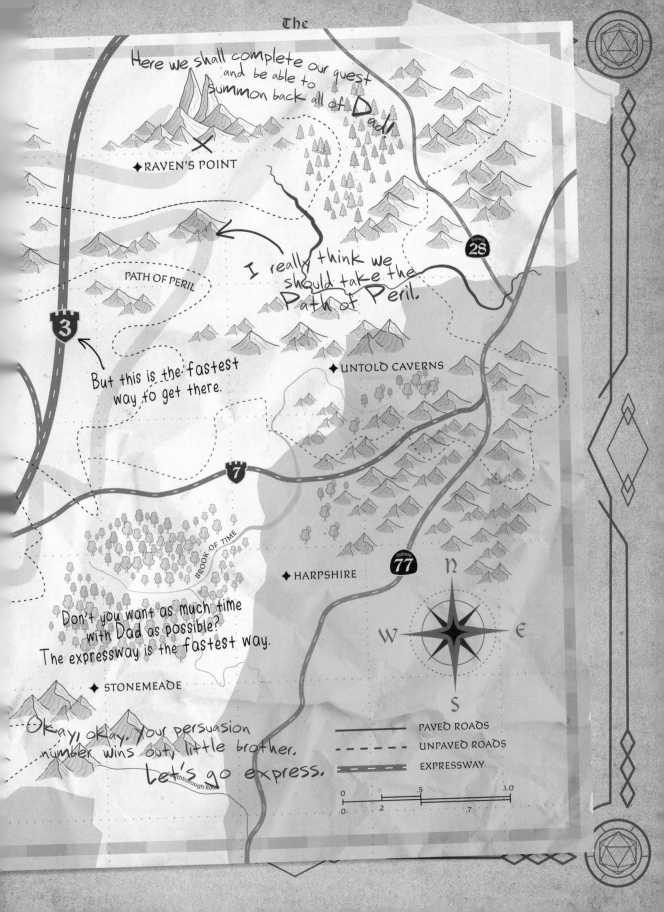

Spells for the Bold Apprentice

You have had your successful meeting with the Manticore and benefited from her wise guidance— your Quest has truly begun!

'Tis time to practice your Magic skills. There's more to a Spell than merely memorizing the Incantations.

PROPER STANCE FOR SPELLCASTIIIING!

Just remember to stay loose, maintain your posture, and...

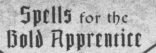

the most important part!
speak from your Heart's Fire! Don't overthink it.
Go on instinct!

Heart's Fire

Magic is nothing to be trifled with, Adventurer!

And unless you speaketh from thy **HEART'S FIRE**, thy Spell will certainly fail. Heart's Fire embodies the following elements:

Purity — You must have good intentions. Magic will not be used for evil or selfish reasons.

Purpose — You must select the correct Spell for the problem at hand.

Passion — You must believe in what you are pursuing. The answer lies inside your heart.

On the pages that follow, you will find your first set of Spells to master as part of becoming a Bold Apprentice.

See? This is what I've been telling you.

I'm trying! But it's not like I can control the answers inside my heart. I don't even have answers inside my head! This is all still a lot of nonsense to me.

HEARTSFIRE

Levitation Spell

When confronted with an object of extraordinary size or weight. When you are trapped in a perilous situation with no hope of escape. In such circumstances, there is no greater friend to the Bold Apprentice than the Levitation Spell.

Aimeth thy staff at the subject of intention, and reciteth this Mystic Incantation:

Aloft Elevar

Was it nonsense when you used this spell in the Manticore's Taver to keep that flaming beam floating in the air? It almost crushed Dad, but you saved him!

It was pretty cool when it worked.
There's something exciting about it.

Casting Magnitude

Die Must Match[*]

str	dur	con	dis
3	2	4	5
str	dur	con	dis
4	3	5	2
str	dur	con	dis
5	4	6	4

[*]using 20-side die

Noteth:

This Spell will only levitate objects a few feet into the air. To reach higher altitudes, use the more advanced Flight Spell.

Speaking of exciting, we're riding Guinevere through the land. She's carrying us on our quest, as valiant as ever! HYAH!

Light Spell

On many occasions, you will be confronted by one of the realm's oldest enemies: darkness. A glowing orb will appear, illuminating even the gloomiest of places. Light your path or home and expel the dark with this Spell.

Aimeth thy staff where you wish there to be light, and reciteth this Mystic Incantation:

Luxia

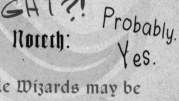

Couldn't you just use a lightbulb for this...?

Lightbulb?

Can a lightbulb dispel A CURSE OF ETERNAL NIGHT?!

Casting Magnitude			
Die Must Match			
str	dur	con	dis
4	3	5	3
str	dur	con	dis
5	4	3	4
str	dur	con	dis
5	6	4	5

†using 20-side die

Noteth:

Probably.

Yes.

Multiple Wizards may be needed to light a great expanse of darkness.

Fog Spell

Sometimes you need to obscure yourself and your path from those who wish to do you harm. With this Spell, a thick fog will roll through the vicinity, clouding the vision of your foes and pursuers.

Twirleth thy staff above thy head, and reciteth this Mystic Incantation:

Cumulo Mystara

This can help us in our continued pursuit of the Phoenix Gem. We may need to conceal ourselves from all manner of monster!

Casting Magnitude

str	dur	con	dis
3	5	4	2
str	dur	con	dis
4	6	5	2
str	dur	con	dis
5	7	3	4

Die Must Match*

*using 20-side die

Noteth:

The Spell is most effective in a still environment. Blustery weather or a Wind Spell can easily blow away the fog.

Velocity Spell

The Summon Spell works best for bringing things near. But what about bringing yourself to far-off things or places? The Velocity Spell will get you there more quickly. Be warned! Only use this spell when the path before you is clear and unobstructed.

Pointeth thy staff in the direction you wish to travel and reciteth this Mystic Incantation:

Accelior

Since we'll need to move quickly, this will probably come in handy at some point!

Casting Magnitude

Die Must Match*

str	dur	con	dis
4	8	5	3
str	dur	con	dis
3	9	6	4
str	dur	con	dis
5	10	4	2

*using 20-side di...

Noteth:

This Spell works best in water, as it will allow you to glide across like a boat.

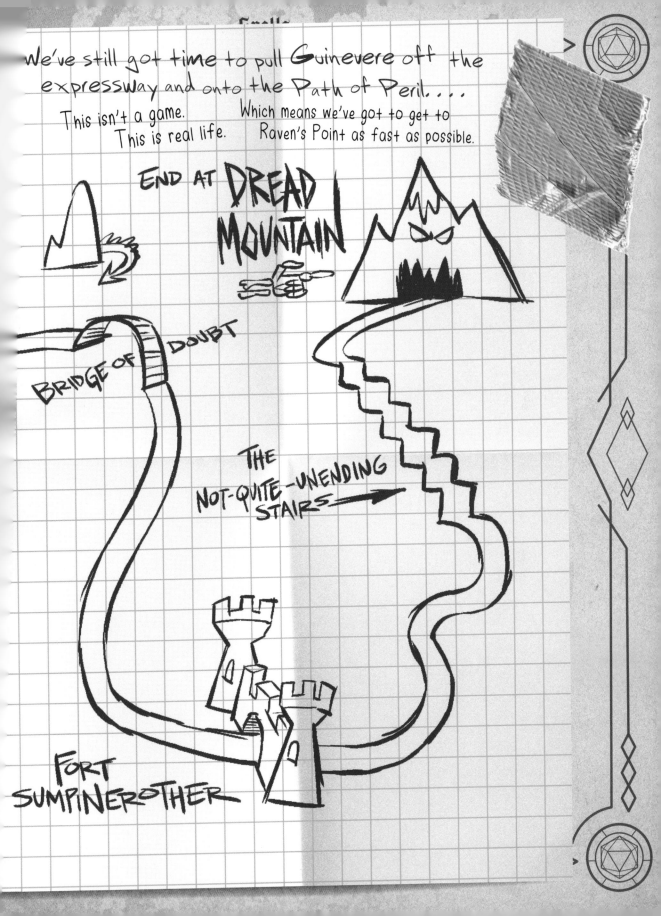

Water Spell

An Adventurer must often go hungry, but you need never go thirsty. This Spell will create an abundance of water—enough to quench the thirst of your whole Questing Party, or to use when the wells run dry in town. This Spell is a popular one to use to aid parched societies the realm over.

Raiseth thy staff above thy head, then strike the end on the ground as you reciteth this Mystic Incantation:

Could use this at home when Barley starts getting especially rank.

Hydro Pura

When adventure awaits, there is no time for something so mundane as a shower. Do you think Faldar cared about his scent while his city was under attack?

Noteth: I don't think so

·Casting Magnitude·

Die Must Match[+]			
str	dur	con	dis
6	4	8	5
str	dur	con	dis
5	4	9	2
str	dur	con	dis
4	3	7	3

[+]using 20-side die

An assist element is needed to conjure waterfalls and other large bodies of water.

Energy Spell

Have you still miles to go before you sleep? Is your mind willing, but your body refusing to budge? The following Spell will give you the assistance you need to put one foot in front of the other, even when sleep is all you desire.

Raiseth thy staff high, and reciteth this Mystic Incantation:

Dimzesta

I'll need this spell the next time I have an all-night campaign!

Casting Magnitude

Die Must Match[+]			
str	dur	con	dis
7	5	8	9
str	dur	con	dis
6	3	10	5
str	dur	con	dis
5	6	9	4

[+]using 20-side die

Noteth:

Although this Spell will provide a surge of energy, it is only temporary. It may wear off in perilous situations!

Fireworks Spell

Fireworks are used in the Questing Realm to signal <u>victory</u> and to signal for help in moments of most dire peril. But for now, let us focus on the positive. This Spell can celebrate a reunion or a homecoming for a Wizard back from their long Quest. Bring together friends, family, and strangers with this dazzling display of lights!

Pointeth thy staff toward the sky and reciteth this Mystic Incantation:

We'll use this spell to signal our glorious victory at the end of the quest.

Boombastia

It'll be the first thing Dad sees when he has fully regenerated!

Casting Magnitude

Die Must Match[+]			
str	dur	con	dis
6	3	4	5
str	dur	con	dis
5	2	3	6
str	dur	con	dis
3	4	5	7

[+]using 20-side die

Noteth:

For an even more spectacular show of fireworks, perform this Spell with a twenty-sided diamond (see page 53).

Unlock Spell

This Spell may appear simple, but hath proven useful in many situations. If a key is not readily available, the Unlock Spell can be a quick and easy solution. Unlock a door that stands in your way, reveal a hidden object, or escape from a trap.

Pointeth thy staff at the lock and reciteth this Mystic Incantation:

Emases Nepo

This would have been super helpful that time I couldn't remember my locker combination.

Casting Magnitude

Die Must Match+			
str	dur	con	dis
5	9	6	7
str	dur	con	dis
4	10	6	5
str	dur	con	dis
3	8	5	4

+using 20-side die

Noteth:

If a lock is enchanted, this simple Spell may not do the trick. It works best on ordinary locks.

Direction Spell

A sense of direction doth not come naturally to all. Sometimes following your feet is the best course to take, but if you have places to go and characters to meet, 'tis best to proceed on the correct route. If you find yourself in an unfamiliar realm, use this Spell to return to the correct path.

When you are in need of guidance, reciteth this Mystic Incantation:

Dad is definitely following his own feet.

Navivera

I must get my keen sense of direction from him!

Casting Magnitude

Die Must Match⁺			
str	dur	con	dis
4	6	5	9
str	dur	con	dis
3	6	5	10
str	dur	con	dis
2	5	3	8

⁺using 20-side die

Noteth:

This Magic is often more reliable than a real compass. Save precious space in your Questing satchel by utilizing the Spell instead.

Wind Spell

This Spell may seem simple, but 'tis no breezy feat to command the Elemental Powers of Nature. To generate even a gentle gust requires intense concentration. This Spell is useful when a sail needs filling, <u>a mane needs drying</u>, or a flame needs coaxing.

Pointeth thy staff at the sky and turn in the shape of a half moon. Then reciteth this Mystic Incantation:

Wynda Zephyria

I think I'll just stick with a hair dryer.

Noteth:

Take heed while performing this Spell. Carelessness can cause the wind to spiral out of control!

Casting Magnitude

Die Must Match[+]			
str	dur	con	dis
8	7	6	5
str	dur	con	dis
9	5	7	6
str	dur	con	dis
10	6	5	7

[+]using 20-side dic

Ian! Read this! These adventures of yore may be the inspiratio you need.

The Tale of Bozark's Hammer

Shields and barriers are useful on a Quest. But be warned—they can also be a hindrance. The tale of Bozark's Hammer illustrates this point.

Disowned by her blacksmith grandfather when she declared her intentions to become a Wizard, Bozark the Centaur sought to escape her family's scorn by scaling the Neverending Wall that separated her home of East Westphalia from its enemy Northwest Southphalia.

Placing a wall between herself and her family brought Bozark no peace. She was shunned by all the Northwest Southphalians except for an elderly Wizard named Razkob the Rebellious, who taught her in the Ways of Magic. Razkob asked what was bringing his pupil so much unhappiness.

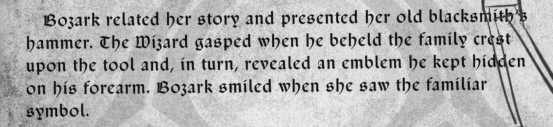

Is that supposed to be me
with the hammer?

Of course!

Bozark related her story and presented her old blacksmith's hammer. The Wizard gasped when he beheld the family crest upon the tool and, in turn, revealed an emblem he kept hidden on his forearm. Bozark smiled when she saw the familiar symbol.

The following day, Bozark declared herself a spy and was put on trial at the foot of the Neverending Wall. People gathered on both sides of the barrier to watch and listen as her fate was decided. When asked to defend herself, she threw her enchanted hammer at the wall. Bozark's Hammer took the wall down in a stupendous shower of stone.

Sweeeeet!

Bozark locked eyes with her stubborn grandfather Zobrak on the other side of the fallen wall. She moved toward him, bringing her teacher Razkob with her. When Zobrak's gaze fell upon the old Wizard, his resolve crumbled. He ran forward and embraced his long-lost cousin Razkob, who had been banished as a boy for practicing magic.

Bozark and her hammer not only reunited her estranged family and countless other families that day, but they reunited an entire nation.

The Tale of Faldar's Horn

Persistence and Vigilance are two traits that will always hold a Young Mage in good stead, as the tale of Faldar's Horn demonstrates.

Faldar the Fantastic was not always known as fantastic. There was a time when he was called "Faldar the Fool." Faldar was born on the Accursed Archipelago—a place of unbridled bounty and boundless joy. In the entire Questing Realm, none were happier than the citizens of this realm. And none among those citizens ever wondered why their land was called "accursed." None except Faldar.

That doesn't make any sense. I'm with Faldar here.

The young Wizard consulted the Elders of the Archipelago and researched the name's origins in the royal library. There seemed to be nothing in his home's history that would earn such a foreboding moniker.

There seemed to Faldar to be only one answer—the name must be a prophecy of future misfortune. His suspicions

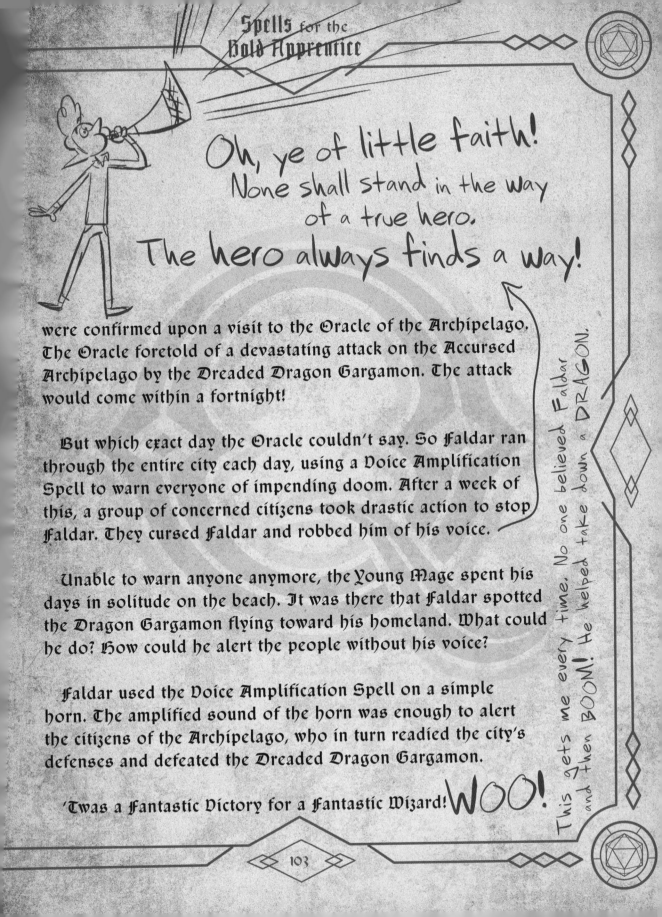

Oh, ye of little faith!
None shall stand in the way of a true hero.
The hero always finds a way!

were confirmed upon a visit to the Oracle of the Archipelago. The Oracle foretold of a devastating attack on the Accursed Archipelago by the Dreaded Dragon Gargamon. The attack would come within a fortnight!

But which exact day the Oracle couldn't say. So Faldar ran through the entire city each day, using a Voice Amplification Spell to warn everyone of impending doom. After a week of this, a group of concerned citizens took drastic action to stop Faldar. They cursed Faldar and robbed him of his voice.

Unable to warn anyone anymore, the Young Mage spent his days in solitude on the beach. It was there that Faldar spotted the Dragon Gargamon flying toward his homeland. What could he do? How could he alert the people without his voice?

Faldar used the Voice Amplification Spell on a simple horn. The amplified sound of the horn was enough to alert the citizens of the Archipelago, who in turn readied the city's defenses and defeated the Dreaded Dragon Gargamon.

'Twas a Fantastic Victory for a Fantastic Wizard! WOO!

This gets me every time. No one believed Faldar, and then BOOM! He helped take down a DRAGON.

The Valiant Mage

You have mastered the beginner Spells and have learned everything necessary for a Bold Apprentice.

'Tis time to take your adventuring to the next step. As a Valiant Mage, one is expected to have mastery over Staff-Wielding Stances as well as Heart's Fire. But do not fear if mastery is still slightly out of reach. Take comfort from such figures as Birdar the Fanciful. Birdar was a promising young Wizard who was not living up to his potential. He much preferred to frolic with Sprites and enjoy nature. But with time, reflection, and experience, Birdar became the honored Wizard that he's known as today.

Regardless of level, do not grow too full of yourself, nor too confident of future success. Your opponents will be more challenging. You will need to learn new Spells to sway them. And those Spells will be more challenging. You can never avoid the challenges of wizardry!

Looks like the author couldn't think of any synonyms for "challenging." How about "difficult," "tough," "tricky," or "taxing"?

Only the bard may determine the precise language of a tale.

The bard knows all!

Alora the Majestic

intimidated ~~challenged~~ by the new ~~challenges~~ trials that lie ahead? Be inspired by the tale of Alora the Majestic.

One cannot describe Alora the Majestic without resorting to superlatives. 'Tis impossible. None could match her brilliance. None could trample her dignity. None could weather her Wizardry.

Even as an Apprentice, she was praised for her intelligence and creativity. As with most Wizards, Magic did not come easily to her, but her natural talents aided her training. These abilities became most useful when Alora came across a firestorm within the quiet town and forest of Crystalwood. It was utter chaos as the villagers tried to escape the flames that had descended upon them. Without hesitation, Alora used her Magic skills as well as clearheaded thinking to save everyone. There was much destruction, but Alora prevented catastrophe.

> Sir Iandore MASTERED that clearheaded thinking! It's the only way we got out of the Manticore's Tavern!

Spells for the Valiant Mage

The same techniques apply to these Spells as Apprentice-level Magic. However, to conjure a successful Spell, one must be even more focused and diligent than ever. 'Tis time to learn about . . . Magic Decrees.

Huh? What's a magic decree?

'Tis easy to feel intimidated by the addition of the Magic Decrees. But fear not! They are merely an additional step for the casting of a Spell (see page 110 for an illustrated example). Maintain focus and remember your practice, and you shall be successful. Understanding Magic Decrees is a vital skill for a Valiant Mage to study before they can progress to Master Wizard.

Be on your guard:

If you do not follow the Magic Decree precisely, there will be unexpected consequences.

Unexpected consequences? That doesn't sound good....

Don't worry.
These spells are the same as the others.
They just have this little extra rule.

Oh boy...

Bad news!
Looks like Guinevere
ran out of gas.

QUEST
RATIONS

She just needs a snack!

But your extra gas can is nearly empty, too!
We don't have much time to figure out where
to find gas and then travel there.

Is there a magic way to get gas?
A gas spell?

If you were complaining about
my "rank" smell earlier, I'm not
sure you'd like a gas spell.

This!

Growth Spell

It's PERFECT!

We'll GROW more gas!

When a Wizard desireth items of diminutive stature to increase in both size and weight, they should look no further than the **Growth Spell**.

Aimeth thy staff at the subject of thy intention, and reciteth this Mystic Incantation:

I don't know about this....

Magnora Bantuan

This is the Magic Decree!

⟨ Casting Magnitude ⟩			
Die Must Match			
str	dur	con	dis
14	20	18	3
str	dur	con	dis
17	8	5	18
str	dur	con	dis
20	15	2	4
*using 20-side die			

Magic Decree
To magnify an object, magnify your attention upon it.

Voice Amplification Spell

This Spell will amplify your voice. 'Tis useful when trying to speak across large distances or to give a rousing speech to your Questing Party.

Place thy staff close to thy mouth, and reciteth this Mystic Incantation:

Vocalys Magnora

I thought we might need this spell because, instead of growing the gas can, I SHRUNK Barley. But he's still plenty loud even when he's tiny.

Casting Magnitude

Die Must Match[+]			
str	dur	con	dis
14	16	19	4
str	dur	con	dis
18	15	14	6
str	dur	con	dis
16	13	12	5

[+]using 20-side die

Magic Decree

To amplify your voice, let your inner voice rise.

It's not my fault the spell backfired. YOU didn't concentrate

I hope we can find a gas station soon. We're going on foot.

Strength Spell

Whether 'tis an impediment blocking your way or an important item you need to bring on your Quest, this Spell will make heavy objects feel as light as a feather.

Place thy staff close to thy arms, and reciteth this Mystic Incantation: *HEY! If you use this spell on me, I'll be able to carry the gas can while we look for a station!*

Might Magnora

*I'll carry the gas can.
And I can just slip you into my pocket.*

*FORGET IT!
I don't need to be carried around!
I'm a GROWN MAN.*

Casting Magnitude

Die Must Match[+]

str	dur	con	dis
16	13	14	6
str	dur	con	dis
18	12	15	5
str	dur	con	dis
15	14	13	7

[+]using 20-side die

Magic Decree

To increase strength, lose the fears that weigh you down.

Fine.

*I hope you can keep up.
We need to find a gas station soon.*

Fire Spell

This Spell will help you create fire to warm a cold night. It can also allow you to see in dark places like dungeons or caves. But be wary, Adventurer, and follow the Magic Decree closely. If you drop your guard, a toasty little fire can flare up into a Quest-ending conflagration without a moment's notice!

Pointeth thy staff and reciteth this Mystic Incantation:

Flame Infernar

Casting Magnitude

Die Must Match+			
str	dur	con	dis
10	17	14	13
str	dur	con	dis
15	16	14	12
str	dur	con	dis
14	13	12	10

+using 20-side die

Magic Decree

Let go of your anger and ire
to ignite the brightest of fire.
Barley is currently in my pocket,
and there's a gas station in sight!
All these delays are just eating away
at our time with Dad.
Hopefully, we'll fill this tank with gas,
get back to the van, and be on our way soon.

Sparkle Sticks are the
sprites' snack of choice!

Music Spell

Music is a form of Magic all on its own. It can soothe better than a Calming Spell. It is even effective in pacifying a savage beast. This Spell is a unifying agent of change throughout the realm. Even the most whimsical Sprite could not create happiness as quickly as this Spell. But you must have a talent for music to unlock its true power.

Circle thy staff
Incantation:

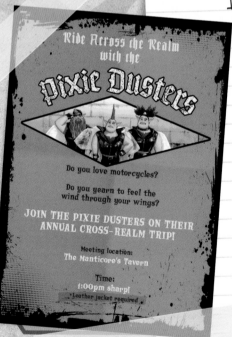

Ride Across the Realm
with the

Pixie Dusters

Do you love motorcycles?

Do you yearn to feel the
wind through your wings?

JOIN THE PIXIE DUSTERS ON THEIR
ANNUAL CROSS-REALM TRIP!

Meeting location:
The Manticore's Tavern

Time:
1:00pm sharp!
*Leather jacket required

I didn't see that coming
with the sprites.

This motorcycle club called
the Pixie Dusters was at
the gas station with us.

They got annoyed with Barley,
and then
Dad accidentally knocked over
their motorcycles.

And then they started

chasing us!

Charm Spell

Music may put an adversary in the mood to listen, but do you have the proper words to sway them to your side? If you have trouble making eye contact and usually trip over your own tongue, 'tis best you use this Spell to give your Charisma score a temporary boost.

Place thy staff by thy mouth and, before you start thy speech, reciteth this Mystic Incantation:

Charismafia

arley was still too small to drive, so I had to do it! It was terrifying.

And drive you did, young mage! Under my wise tutelage, you skillfully steered through traffic and eluded the sprites!

- Casting Magnitude -

Die Must Match[+]			
str	dur	con	dis
8	15	16	9
str	dur	con	dis
12	14	15	10
str	dur	con	dis
13	12	17	11

[+]using 20-side die

Magic Decree

A friendly smile is the best to persuade even the most obstinate foes.

Disguise Spell

This Spell will create the illusion that you are someone else. 'Tis perfect for creating a distraction, eluding guards, or deceiving those who will impede your noble Quest.

Pass thy staff across thy own body, and reciteth this Mystic Incantation:

Illusio Facadis

On the bright side, I'm REGULAR SIZE AGAIN!
But we have a teeny problem: my wallet.
It's still tiny. And we just got pulled over by the cops.
But look at this tiny gift card!
Fries are on me when this grows back.

Casting Magnitude

Die Must Match[+]			
str	dur	con	dis
13	15	17	10
str	dur	con	dis
14	16	18	11
str	dur	con	dis
12	17	16	12

[+]*using 20-side die*

Magic Decree

Disguising yourself is a lie, so you must tell the truth to get by.

We'll use this Disguise Spell to pretend to be someone the cops will def-- ...

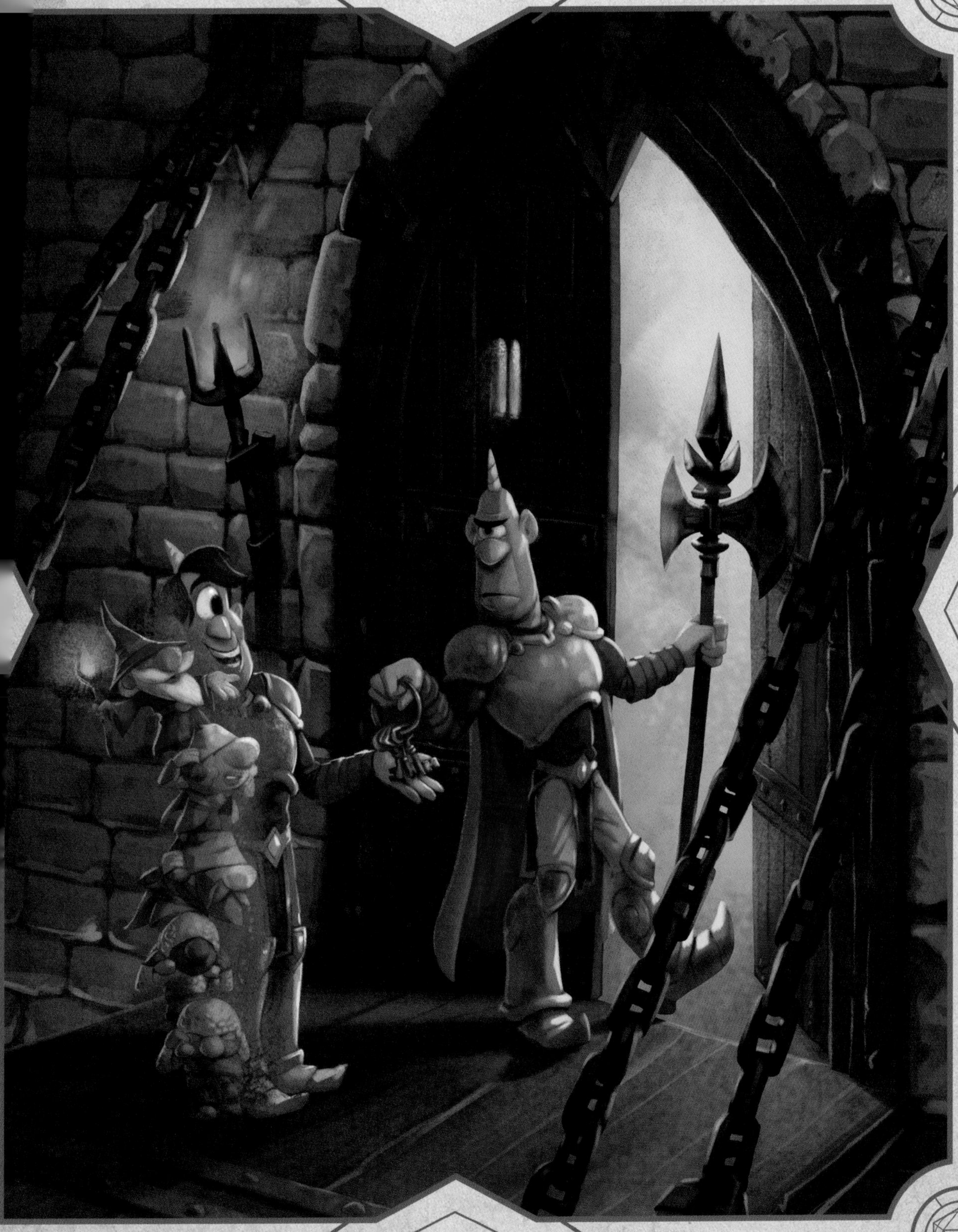

Calming Spell

Yeou must be prepared to calm those who would threaten you or endanger the completion of your Quest. But you may also use this Spell to calm your shaken comrades or new friends.

Wave thy staff slowly in front of thy eyes, and reciteth this Mystic Incantation:

Tranquilara

I should've used this Calming Spell instead of the Disguise Spell.
The disguise worked as long as I told the truth.
But when the cops called Barley a screwup and I tried to disagree…

-Casting Magnitude-			
Die Must Match‡			
str	dur	con	dis
12	14	15	11
str	dur	con	dis
13	15	14	12
str	dur	con	dis
16	13	17	10

‡using 20-side die

Magic Decree

Find quiet and peace
so that discord may cease.

I started to transform
back into myself.
And Barley noticed.

Shield Spell

Protect thyself from barbs, arrows, and all manner of deadly weapons. This Spell can be useful when encountering traps and enemies during thy Quest.

Hold thy staff out in front of you, and reciteth this Mystic Incantation:

Bastion Fortigar

I've tried to explain, but Barley isn't speaking to me.
It's really awkward.

Casting Magnitude

str	dur	con	dis
14	15	13	10
str	dur	con	dis
16	13	17	11
str	dur	con	dis
13	16	15	12

Die Must Match[+]

+using 20-side die

Magic Decree

An unblinking stare is required if a strong barrier is desired.

Healing Spell

This Spell will heal minor wounds and other damage earned in battle. Alas, 'tis not effective for emotional damage. If you have accidentally hurt someone on your own team, 'tis best to speak from the heart and to heal it

Barley and I had this big fight about how I didn't listen to him.

And that I didn't listen to him because I didn't think he had good ideas.

But then an amazing thing happened....

Dad started dancing.

The music from Barley's van was super loud so Dad must have felt the vibrations through his feet.

Now I know where I get MY bad dancing from.

I don't think we could call it dancing.

I've never seen anything like that before.

But you had some sweet moves, little brother!

We decided to do things Barley's way. We're taking the Path of Peril. I hope this works!

Trust me, it'll work! ONWARD TO THE PATH OF PERIL!

Summon Spell

I wish!

Ever been pinned under a Dragon's claw with thy sword just out of reach? Or been trapped in the corner by a deadly Giant Spider while thy rope is across the cavern? Then you know the usefulness of the Summon Spell. Remember: the Summon Spell only works with items that you can actually see in front of you at the time of summoning.

No thanks!

Aimeth thy staff at the object you need, and repeat this Mystic Incantation:

Conjurus

Even Dad left his mark on the book!

Casting Magnitude

Die Must Match

str	dur	con	dis
	16	11	12
str	dur	con	dis
15	13	11	14
str	dur	con	dis
15	14	12	1

tng 204 dc 8c

Magic Decree

The image in thy mind must be clear of the true object

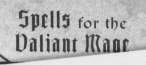

Oooh,
I remember this campaign!
This was an all-nighter for us.

The Tale of
Yaldina's Quest

Me and my heroic comrades had reached an impasse on our mighty journey! The ancient bronze Elder Skeleton guarded the Chalice of Charity, but my troupe and I feared not! For Wardus had a heart of courage and fire! And Yaldina whispered words using the Charm Spell to trick the garish guard. We snuck past him and, with good in our hearts, took the chalice from its perch and returned it to its rightful place.

I don't know where Barley keeps all this information in that brain of his.

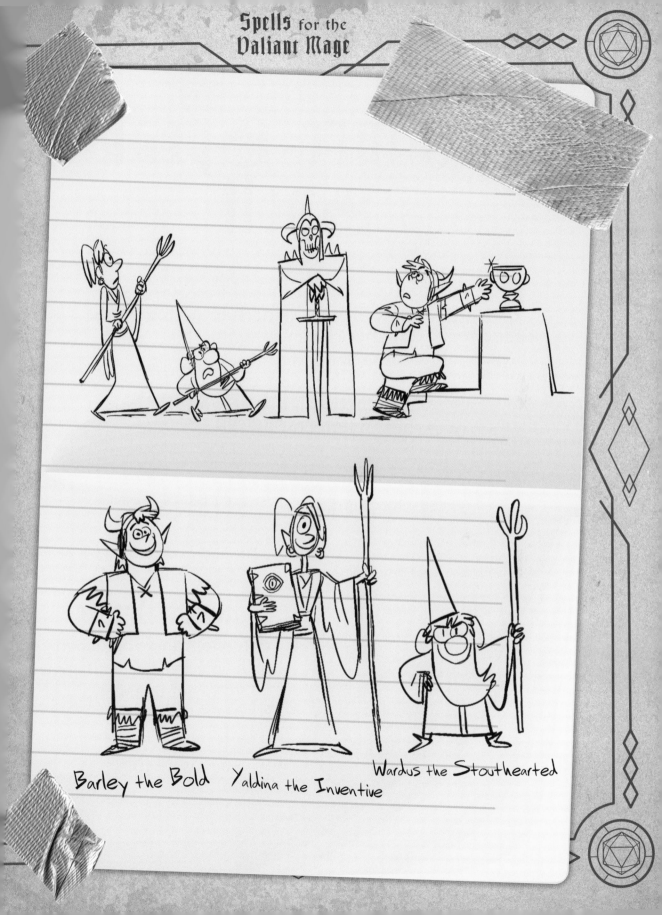

Barley the Bold   Yaldina the Inventive   Wardus the Stouthearted

Nature Speak Spell

Are you trying to aid an injured creature? Are you in need of forest critters to help with the housework? Use this charm to understand and speak to the beasts around you.

Place thy staff in between thyself and the animal, then reciteth this Mystic Incantation:

Bestia Lingu

We should use this spell to talk to Blazey!
I've always wondered what she thinks about.

Casting Magnitude

Die Must Match+			
str	dur	con	dis
12	15	13	19
str	dur	con	dis
11	13	14	18
str	dur	con	dis
14	13	16	15

+using 20-side die

Magic Decree

Before opening your mouth, open your mind to a different way of thinking.

Translation Spell

O ftentimes, it may seem simpler to speak to thy
steed than to converse with someone from
a strange land. Nothing could be further from
the truth! The Translation Spell will remove all
misunderstandings and bridge any cultural divides.

Politely pointeth the tip of thy staff at the
stranger's ear and the bottom at thy own mouth,
then reciteth this Mystic Incantation:

Universa Lingu

Casting Magnitude

Die Must Match[+]			
str	dur	con	dis
10	13	15	19
str	dur	con	dis
13	14	15	16
str	dur	con	dis
13	12	16	17

[+]using 20-side die

Magic Decree

Compassion is most important
to understand all speech
around you.

Trust Bridge Spell

orges, crevasses, pits both bottomed and bottomless — the Questing Realm is filled with large empty spaces that you will need to traverse. Not to worry! This Spell will create an invisible bridge across any gaping, deadly abyss.

Gaping?

Deadly?

Walk out onto nothing with confidence as you reciteth this Mystic Incantation:

Bridgrigar Invisia

I'm not sure about this Path of Peril. Barley has driven us to the edge of a bottomless pit. There's a bridge, but the lever is on the other side. So Barley wants me to cross the pit using this spell!

⸙ Casting Magnitude ⸙

str	dur	con	dis
16	15	17	13
str	dur	con	dis
15	16	14	12
str	dur	con	dis
17	14	16	14

Die Must Match⁺

⁺using 20-side die

Magic Decree

Believe in yourself with every step, and you will never slip.

There has got to be another way.

The Tale of the Shield of Zadar

How do you trust someone

Here are some ideas of how to cross the pit.

...lation Island
...r anything.
...been
...attacks, and
...iant Cyclops
...ey

But I think this will take too long.

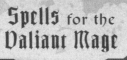

Well, I went along with Barley's foolproof plan....
I mean, it wasn't much of a plan. Just a rope tied around my
waist and some words of encouragement. But that rope DID save
me from plunging into the Bottomless Pit when I didn't trust
enough in the Trust Bridge Spell the first time. And after that,
I wasn't really afraid of falling. I don't know exactly why.

My brother's got MAD MAGICAL SKILLS!
He didn't even need the rope I had tied around his waist.
Just look at this awesome mage!

The rope slipped off when
I was only a few feet out???
Thank you for not telling me.

Nah, it slipped off right in the middle!

The Tale of the Tooth of Zadar

Things are not always as they seem. 'Tis a good lesson for every Adventurer, young and old. And the tale of the Tooth of Za illustrates the point

It turns out that we weren't supposed to go to Raven's Point at all.
After Ian lowered the bridge, we noticed a raven statue that was pointing to another raven in the distance. The ravens are _pointing_ us toward the gem!

We would've gone the wrong way if we took the expressway like I had said. I should've trusted Barley's gut.

MY GUT KNOWS ALLLLLL!

Well, maybe not all, but I ha

Okay, so I tried to listen to my gut, and apparently my gut is perpetually WRONG because it got us involved in a high-speed chase with the cops.

Eh, it was just Colt.

I've gotten in trouble with him tons of times. But then a bunch of OTHER cops showed up.

My brother is a REBEL GONE ROGUE! A ROGUE rogue!

We didn't have time to be hauled back to town! We had no choice but to jump into Guinevere and drive away.

Later, I tried to do the Arcane Lightning Spell and use it to block the road behind us with boulders. But I wasn't strong enough. So instead, Barley drove Guinevere into the cliffside to create a barricade. I don't know what to say.

Fallen Comrades

'Tis [...]ful truth of the Questing Realm. [...] member of your team will see

BRAVE GUINEVERE

We were facing our darkest hour.
Besieged by opponents! Trapped with no hope of escape!

You drove forth and sacrificed
yourself to save us!

She is gone too soon,
cut down in her prime.
But now, you ride with
the angels,
sweet
Guinevere.

May you park in the
halls of Valhalla.

Eat, Drink, and Be Merry!

She was a good girl.

And be sure to get an oil change because
you are long overdue.

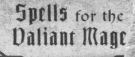

Your sacrifice has
not been in vain, ol'gal!
At long last,
we have found the path to the
PHOENIX GEM!

We followed the directions of all the
raven statues. But the last statue
pointed down at a disc in the ground.
The disc reflected a stone in the
raven's chest. It looked like this:

This is DEFINITELY it, little brother!
The wavy lines indicate water.
The X is the Phoenix Gem!
We follow the water into the tunnel
and it takes us to the gem.
SIMPLE.

But we don't know how far the river goes or
how long it will take us to get to the end.
So, if we are going to do this,
we need to move QUICKLY.

Inventive Spellcastin

A crucial test lies ahead of you, Adventurer!
Many chall

Ian has got this covered!
We needed a boat for our trip down the river,
and we needed to move fast.
BOOM! Sir Iandore used a Growth Spell
with a Velocity Spell.

It was Barley's brilliant and bizarre idea to create
a boat from an enlarged CHEESE PUFF!

On a quest, you gotta use what you have.
Told you cheese puffs were essential!

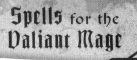
It was pretty cool.
I was trying out all kinds of spells.

Growth! BOOOOOP!

Velocity! ZOOM!

Fireworks!
KAPOW!
cracklecracklecrackle

Levitation!
SWOOOOOP!

I finally feel like I could be the
Valiant Mage that this book is talking about.

That's what I've been saying.
You're a natural!
But not just a Valiant Mage . . .
A MASTER WIZARD.

Quest Secrets

What lies hidden behind that door? 'Tis a riddle easily solved with powerful arms or powerful Magic.

But 'tis a far tougher task to find what lies hidden in a person's soul.

Be careful! Untold Secrets can tear apart even the closest cadre of Adventurers.

This book is right once again!
I had an untold secret gnawing at me.

I've always told Ian that
I had only three memories of Dad.

But there's a fourth memory.

When Dad was sick ...
I was supposed to go in and say
goodbye to him. But he was hooked
up to all these tubes and ...
he didn't look like himself.
I got scared.
And I didn't go in.

But that's when I decided:
I was never gonna be scared again.
And look at me now.

I'm glad you told me.

Okay, I may have broken my vow. We just went through a SUPER SCARY 👁👁👁 series of deadly traps! 👁👁👁 We had ended our trip down the river and reached ... THE FINAL GAUNTLET!

There was this ancient archway and all these symbols everywhere. I wish I knew what they meant.

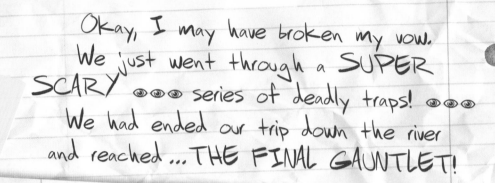

We barely had time to marvel at our surroundings when, suddenly, a blade shot out from the wall and sliced poor Dad in half!

Luckily, it only took off the top half with the disguise. But that was close!

Then we encountered the most horrifying thing in the Questing Realm.
It was the dreaded cube!
It was just as green, slimy, and gelatinous as I imagined!

The hideous monster swallowed Dad's disguise.
It quickly dissolved to nothing!

And then the relentless goo pursued us down a passage.
I thought we needed to figure out some kind of puzzle,
but Barley told me to grab a shield. We surrounded Dad and
sprinted down the passage as ACTUAL axes, swords, and
arrows shot at us from every which way.

We made it to the other side, but then we
discovered a pit of spikes! But Sir Iandore used
his awesome skills to magic us over the pit!

We escaped the tunnel . . . only to find ourselves in a chamber
that started filling up with water! Like adventurers in the crux
of their quest, we were going to drown!

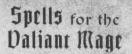

But a glimmer of hope appeared in the form of an underwater release valve! And lo! Who could hold their breath long enough to swim down there and trigger it?

Our dad, that's **who!**

We used Dad's leash to direct him to the tile. When he stepped on it, the water stopped rising!

Look at that father and son **teamwork!** This is the kind of unity that questing parties can only dream of!

The Phoenix **Gem** awaits beyond this door!

Shall we?

We certainly shall!

We have followed the quest, and it has led us to our victory!

Reversals of Fortune

reversals of fortune for us!   Only fortune and success!

The only certainty on a Quest is uncertainty, Adventurer. It seems you are on the brink of success when, suddenly, Fate deals an unfortunate hand. Your plans may have failed, you may have encountered unexpected setbacks, or you may be left alone without your Questing Party.

These reversals of fortune are enough to disband even the strongest of parties. Some fellowships can only withstand times of certainty and will quickly disintegrate at the first sign of struggle. But 'tis impossible to execute a perfect Campaign. Trials are inevitable regardless of an Adventurer's level of experience. So fear not—all hope is not lost. How quickly you recover is up to you.

The Master Wizard

How dost thou fare, Adventurer? Have you embodied the skills and strength of the Mage? Has Questing been more challenging than you imagined? Are you bleary-eyed and battle-worn like a Mighty Warrior, or a Garrulous Bard whose voice has tired from singing the land over? And is what you now most desire to kick up your feet in front of a stout fire? Aye! But there is more to learn! The realm is full of troubles that need tending to. Better to meet them head-on. Better to continue on your path to become a Master Wizard.

Now that you have reached the level of Master Wizard, casting Spells becomes all the more difficult. The Magic Decrees are even more veiled, the Spellcasting positions even more complex.

Your focus and dedication must be impenetrable, especially when facing imminent danger. Do not let down your guard or become too complacent. Even the most seasoned Wizards may falter in life-or-death situations. One never grows out of the need for discipline.

Gird your eyes and steel your heart!
For great peril lies ahead!
But also great opportunities to create a more prosperous realm for all . . .

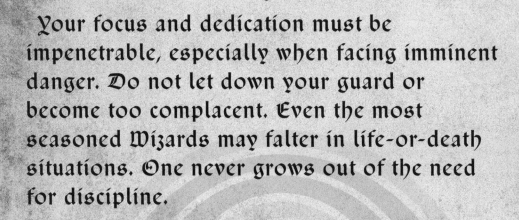

I can't BELIEVE what just happened.
I'm so upset.

Me and Barley got out of the tunnel and ended up right where we started: smack-dab in the middle of downtown New Mushroomton.

The Phoenix Gem must be at Raven's Point, which we could've been at <u>hours</u> ago! I should have followed my head, not my gut, and kept us on the expressway. But I let Barley lead us because I felt bad for calling him a screwup.

Well, he IS a screwup.
And he's screwed up my one chance to meet Dad.

Shamblefoot the Wondrous

I don't know why I'm reading this stupid book. It has all been completely pointless.

Nonsense is right.

This Wizard had a curious but effective way of facing troubles head-on. Shamblefoot bumbled around the countryside, alternating between spouting mystical nonsense and playing his flute.

Why, then, is this eccentric character the epitome of a Master Wizard? Many a Bard has told the tale of Shamblefoot's three apprentices. They set out on an adventure to seek the Great Relic. In the Fiery Swamp, the first apprentice fled after fire began to close around them. In the Stupefying Storm, the second took cover as the winds howled.

The last apprentice followed Shamblefoot through swamps, storms, and finally, the Winding Labyrinth. They wandered the maze all winter, singing and dancing along the way. In spring, Shamblefoot said, "You have persevered, and now we have found the relic: Heart's Fire. 'Tis here," he said, touching his chest. "For a Master Wizard does not seek treasures or relics of power. Instead, they seek charity, understanding, and peace."

I'm sitting in the park with Dad as the sun is beginning to set.

Zantar the Great

Zantar is the most celebrated Master Wizard in the Questing Realm. But she was not always such. There was no one who tried harder to learn Magic than young Zantar. She spent endless hours studying every Spell book she could find. But she was still only mediocre.

In her darkest hour, Zantar stumbled upon a strange old mage playing a flute along with his two young apprentices. This was Shamblefoot, and Zantar became his third apprentice. Shamblefoot showed Zantar that there was more to Magic than memorized Spells and proper stances. She found the humor, joy, and passion one needs to become a true Master Wizard.

After parting ways with Shamblefoot, Zantar found herself embroiled in the Battle of Siren Song. With ships sailing toward battle, Zantar rowed out in a boat between the two camps, raised her staff, and recited a Spell that ended the war. Zantar had invented her very own Spell: Arcane Lightning (see page 167), which is considered to be one of the most difficult Spells a Wizard can master. It lit up the sky, illuminating the truth that Unity should prevail over Discord.

Time's almost up.

I wish I got the chance to know Dad's kind of humor, what brings him joy, and what he's passionate about. I wonder if he'd tell really bad Dad jokes. Kinda like the ones that Barley is always cracking.

Spells for the Master Wizard

Now you are ready to begin your Spellcasting as a Master Wizard. These Spells are not only ideal for personal defense ~~during~~ but many will also

- ☑ ~~Play catch~~
- ☑ ~~Take a walk~~
- ☑ ~~Heart to heart~~
- ☑ ~~Laugh together~~
- ☑ ~~Driving lesson~~
- ☑ Share my life with him

Barley can be pretty funny, and he's always super passionate about magic and history.

And he's the most joyful person I know.

I realized I've done all these things from my list...with Barley.

I never had a dad, but I had my brother.

He was always there for me.
He picked me up when I was down.

He's always seen the best in things... including in me.

What I've been needing my whole life,

I got through Barley.

Stun Spell

This Spell will temporarily stun any oncoming threat. The duration of the Spell depends on your abilities as a Wizard, and the size and strength of the threat. An Apprentice can stun a wasp for an hour, but it takes a Master to stop a Dragon for a minute.

Pointeth thy staff at the threat, then jab with it, and reciteth this Mystic Incantation:

Paralos

I never should have called Barley
a screwup. I've got to find him.

Casting Magnitude

Die Must Match[+]			
str	dur	con	dis
16	14	17	15
str	dur	con	dis
17	16	18	14
str	dur	con	dis
15	17	16	13

[+]using 20-side die

Magic Decree

Praise your foe
so they cannot go.

Gravity Inversion Spell

Unlike the Levitation Spell, the Gravity Inversion Spell can undo the laws of gravity in the immediate area around you. Your foes will fall UP!

Spin thy staff above thy head while slowly raising your voice. Then reciteth this Mystic Incantation:

Contragrava

Casting Magnitude

str	dur	con	dis
16	17	18	15
str	dur	con	dis
14	16	17	13
str	dur	con	dis
15	18	16	12

Die Must Match[+]

+using 20-side die

Magic Decree

You must be grounded in body and mind if you want to leave the ground behind.

Danger Detection Spell

Danger does not always come rushing at you. Sometimes it hides in plain sight. Sometimes it sneaks up on you when your guard is down. This Spell highlights hidden enemies and threats.

Spin with thy staff out in front of you. Then reciteth this Mystic Incantation:

No danger detection for us when we battled AN ACTUAL DRAGON.

Exposa Hazadir

It was EPIC! It was COLOSSAL! It was a BATTLE for the AGES!

Casting Magnitude

Die Must Match+			
str	dur	con	dis
13	16	15	18
str	dur	con	dis
15	14	13	17
str	dur	con	dis
15	18	16	12

+using 20-side die

Magic Decree

Only a mind at peace will know that which lurks in the shadows below.

And the greatest treasure of all lay in sight at the quest's end: the chance for Ian and me to talk to Dad, one last time.

Armor Spell

An effective way to reduce damage in any advanced Quest. This Spell will harden and toughen your skin so that weapons and high-level Spells cannot get to you. The armor encapsulates you like a suit of <u>invisible chain mail.</u> But this Spell requires immense concentration and only lasts a short while.

Touch the tip of the staff from one shoulder to the other, and reciteth this Mystic Incantation:

Armadura

This spell would've come in handy! Saving it for next time.

Casting Magnitude

str	dur	con	dis
Die Must Match*			
17	18	19	13
str	dur	con	dis
16	19	20	14
str	dur	con	dis
15	17	18	12

*using 20-side die

Magic Decree

Words of others must be rejected for you to remain protected.

Truth Spell

This Spell encourages honesty. It will persuade your good friends or even perfect strangers to tell the hard truth. Take care in how you phrase your questions, however. Vague or open-ended questions may create confusion for the subject.

Wave thy staff in a wide arc around the person before you. Then maintain eye contact, and reciteth this Mystic Incantation:

Trüstavera

Casting Magnitude

Die Must Match[+]			
str	dur	con	dis
13	15	16	18
str	dur	con	dis
15	14	16	20
str	dur	con	dis
13	15	14	18

[+]using 20-side die

Magic Decree

Be true to yourself
to bring truth out of others.

Sir Iandore and Sir Barley
and the
Slaying of the Dragon Curse of New Mushroomton

It all started simply enough: Sir Barley was at his lowest point. There was no Phoenix Gem. His questing party was gone. He was alone and believed his quest for the ages had failed. THEN, in a stunning display of insight, he realized that the stone they had found on the Path of Peril was really the KEY to finding the Phoenix Gem!

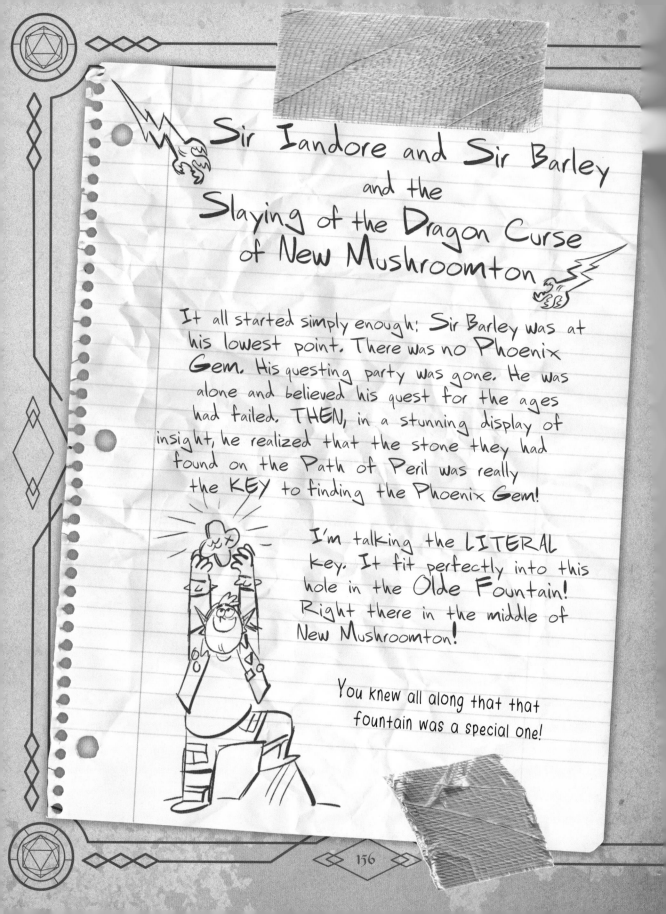

I'm talking the LITERAL key. It fit perfectly into this hole in the Olde Fountain! Right there in the middle of New Mushroomton!

You knew all along that that fountain was a special one!

When Sir Barley put the stone
key into place, something
AMAZING happened.

LO AND BEHOLD . . .

THE PHOENIX GEM

At this point, Sir Barley's trusty
questing party had returned.
He knew he could always count on Sir Iandore.

I was really sorry for calling you a screwup, Barley.
You were right the whole time. You hadn't led us astray.

Light Beam Spell

This Spell is not to be confused with the Light Spell. While the Light Spell is ideal for illuminating a room or finding a path, the Light Beam Spell creates powerful rays that have the ability to banish darkness from an entire cave, temporarily obscure an enemy's sight, or even crack boulders.

With immense force, drive the staff into the ground and command this Mystic Incantation:

Luxia Extraordinar

Casting Magnitude

Die Must Match+			
str	dur	con	dis
18	16	17	15
str	dur	con	dis
17	15	18	13
str	dur	con	dis
16	14	15	17

+using 20-side die

Magic Decree

Imagine lightness of mind and send it forth with fortitude.

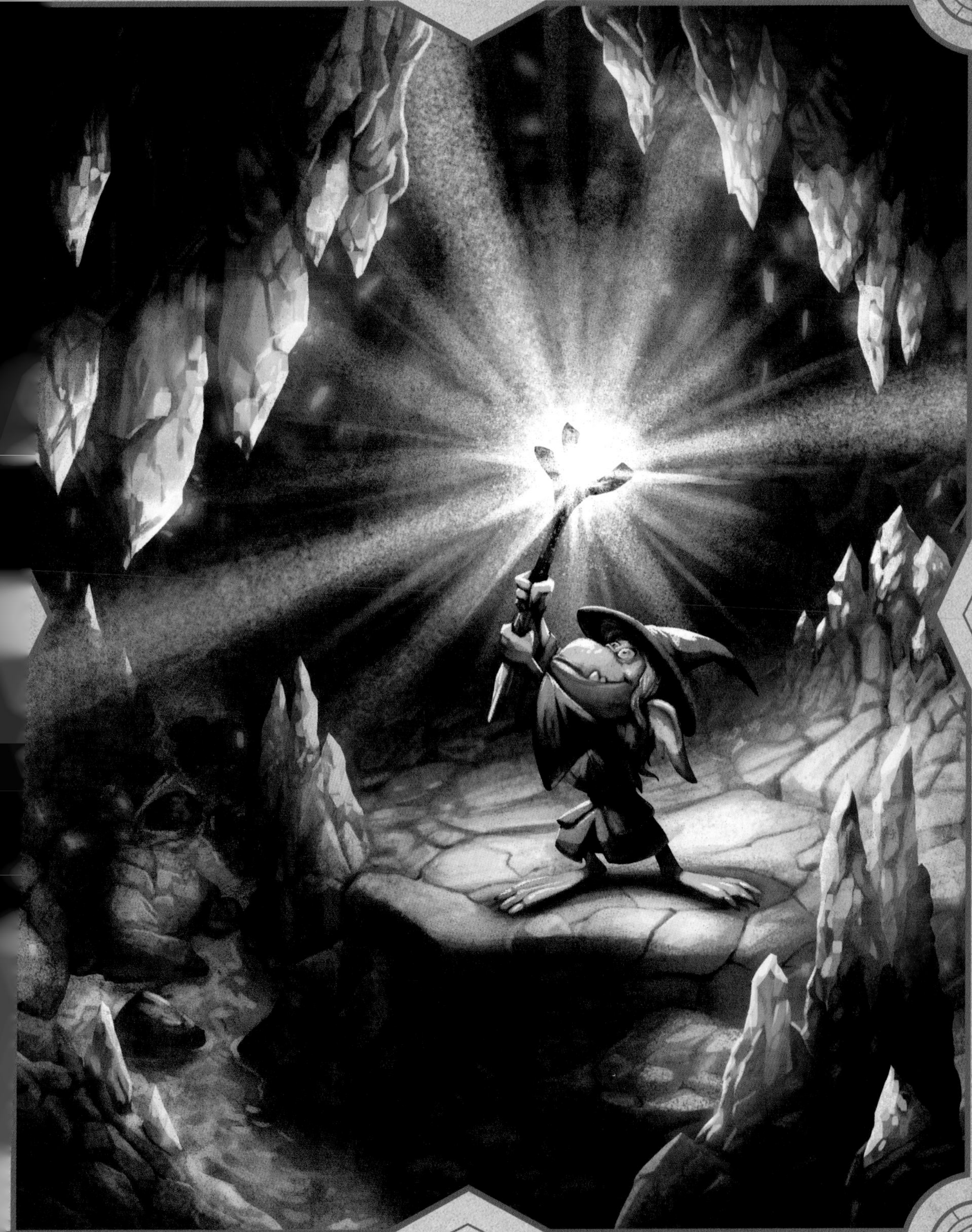

Here's where things got truly epic.
Unbeknownst to brave Sir Barley, a curse ca
creeping out of the Olde Fountain and star
tearing apart the high school!

Sir Iandore and Dad make
their triumphant return!

Sorry we're late!

All the parts came together to form:
THE DRAGON CURSE! And then . . .

mmm. Maybe it'd just be easier to draw it out.

This is basically what happened:

m swoops in on the Manticore?!
What a twist!

Dragon's hungry
for this beauty.

Dragon Curse doesn't know it, but he's about to meet
THE CURSE CRUSHER!

Flight Spell

You may think this is merely the Levitation Spell, but that is a dangerous misconception. The Flight Spell provides control and speed that the Levitation Spell does not. However, the Spell will fail if one soars too high or too far.

Tap the base of thy staff into the ground, then swiftly point the staff skyward as you reciteth this Mystic Incantation:

Avi Volanta

⬥ Casting Magnitude ⬥

Die Must Match*			
str	dur	con	dis
16	20	17	15
str	dur	con	dis
15	19	18	16
str	dur	con	dis
14	18	17	15

*using 20-side die

Magic Decree

To soar through the sky,
tell your heavy burdens goodbye.

Mom and the Manticore already
had the flying part covered!

Animate Spell

This Spell will cause inanimate objects to walk about and do as you command. Very useful if you have been tied up and left to rot by a crafty Rogue, or if you are trying to entertain your comrades by the campfire.

Aimeth thy staff at the subject of thy intention, then draw the shape of a heart in the air. Tap it in the center, and reciteth this Mystic Incantation:

Presto Avar

Casting Magnitude

Die Must Match[+]			
str	dur	con	dis
15	17	16	14
str	dur	con	dis
16	18	17	15
str	dur	con	dis
15	16	18	13

[+]using 20-side die

Magic Decree

Only when you breathe in and out will things begin to move about.

Invisibility Spell

We have all wanted to figuratively make ourselves disappear when suffering embarrassment or getting scolded. This Spell will literally do the job, rendering you or anyone you wish invisible. 'Tis also useful when trying to sneak past guards and other foes.

Pointeth thy staff at thyself or another, draw a triangle in the air with the tip of the staff and gesture a slash through it, then reciteth this Mystic Incantation:

This is my drawing of Sir Iandore performing the Invisibility Spell!

Visage Invisio

Magic Decree.
To go unnoticed,
you must appear to belong.

◆ Casting Magnitude ◆			
Die Must Match✝			
str	dur	con	dis
15	16	18	14
str	dur	con	dis
16	20	19	15
str	dur	con	dis
14	15	20	16

✝using 20-side die

Stone Spell

An inanimate object can become as sturdy as stone with this Incantation. This can prove useful when trying to create a hefty barricade, or to create sturdier dwelling walls for your lean-to.

Aimeth thy staff at the subject of thy intention, draw a circle in the air, then bring the staff down hard into the ground and reciteth this Mystic Incantation:

Petrifor

Magic Decree

Show fortitude in your decisions and you will be unbreakable.

Casting Magnitude

Die Must Match[+]			
str	dur	con	dis
20	19	18	16
str	dur	con	dis
19	18	17	20
str	dur	con	dis
18	20	17	15

[+]using 20-side die

Arcane Lightning

W hen a Wizard desires to obliterate or explode items into the smallest of particles, then look no further than the ancient Spell of Arcane Lightning. One must take care, as this is one of if not *the* most dangerous and powerful Spells known to Wizardom.

If you are prepared, keep thine eyes on the clouds and thy hands tightly around thy staff, and reciteth this Mystic Incantation:

Voltar Thundasir

This spell has nothing on Sir Iandore! Ian, you gotta tell the rest of the story!

Casting Magnitude

Die Must Match+			
str	dur	con	dis
19	18	20	16
str	dur	con	dis
17	20	19	18
str	dur	con	dis
20	18	19	17

+using 20-side die

Magic Decree

To make lightning strike with ease, one must follow all decrees.

Battling Monsters

'Tis a weighty subject that we must now tackle. We Quest to become our best selves and bring benefit to the realm. But there will be occasions where you will find yourself Battling Monsters.

So, there we were: Me, Barley, Mom, and the Manticore, all battling the Dragon Curse of New Mushroomton.

Mom and the Manticore attacked the dragon, but it swatted them out of the sky.

But then Mom came back to the rescue, sticking part of the Manticore's sword, the Curse Crusher, into the dragon's core, which temporarily stunned it.

Ian and I made it to the top of the hill.
And that's when Ian finally cast the
Visitation Spell that brought Dad to life.

I thought it was going to fail again, but then
Barley braced me as the rest of Dad began to materialize.

The dragon still wanted the Phoenix Gem, and it was willing to
spoil our family reunion to get it. I fought off the dragon,
reciting the spells I'd learned. All of us were working together
to give Barley and Dad their moment together.

I still don't know how to thank you.

This was your one chance to say goodbye.
There's no way I was going to let you give that up.

Vanquish the monsters that cros

The Story of Gargamon's Tail

I did all I could to give Barley time with Dad.
I wielded magic, casting spells left and right
to keep the dragon at bay.

As glad as I am to have had my moment with Dad,
I sure wish I also got to see you in action.

It was like the spells just came to me.
I didn't have to think about which one to use next.
I used all the best ones:

☑ Trust Bridge Spell

☑ Fireworks Spell

☑ Levitation Spell

☑ Growth Spell

☑ Velocity Spell

☑ Arcane Lightning

It was awesome.

It was like when Zantar seemed like this average wizard at first, but after practicing and building her confidence, she became one of the most renowned wizards in history.

I have no words. . . .
You are a **LEGEND!**

I'd do it all again, too.
The risk was worth it.

Spoken like a true wizard!

The Tale of Chantar's Talon

Fortunes will rise and fall and rise again through every Quest and every lifetime as the Tale of Chantar's Talon so poignantly demonstrates. The Noble Dragon Chantar was Lord of the Skies in Skyehaven, and it took a keen interest in what happened on the land.

The beast decided to help the orphans of Skyehaven. It dug up   to give them, breaking off   process. The orphans Talon a talisman of g   as carefully as the gol

And then one day, th they feared their goo

I was so nervous, but I asked the Manticore if she'd write a little something for the book.

Universal
Runic Wheel

The Manticore

But she didn't write a little something.
She wrote a BIG something.
SHE AUTOGRAPHED MY BOOK!
I'm going to treasure this page forever.

The Conclusion

Now that you have learned what is required for a successful Campaign, there is but one lesson to leave you with, Adventurer: aiding those in need is more important than any treasure or glory that a Quest may bring. A Wizard discovers faith in themselves, embodies the spirit of selflessness, and uses their Heart's Fire for others.

I'm really curious about how Mom and the Manticore teamed up and arrived for battle.

Yes!

Share your knowledge, Laurel the Mighty Warrior! How did you get the Curse Crusher? Sir Barley and Sir Iandore (politely) command you!

I followed you boys to the tavern and saved the Manticore from police questioning after the fire incident. I mean, it was her tavern. If she wanted to change it up and start fresh, I don't see how that's the police's business. And no one got hurt. We simply drove away and I observed all speed limits while doing so.

But the Manticore told me about the Phoenix Gem curse, so I had to do something to help. Which reminds me: please kindly inform me the next time you two decide to go on a quest that threatens life and limb. Your anxious mother would greatly appreciate it.

And we retrieved the Manticore's sword from a pawn shop of all places. But it was all the Manticore's idea to paralyze the goblin shop owner with a sting from her scorpion tail. I had nothing to do with that. Thankfully, the venom in the Manticore's tail only lasts for about an hour. AND it was totally justified because the goblin changed the once reasonable price to an OUTRAGEOUS price in order for us to buy

back the Curse Crusher sword, which was never going to happen. So, I left some money on the counter, we grabbed the sword, and we ran out of there.

And yes, we ran into the same motorcycle club as you boys. As I explained before, that's how I crashed my car. And no, that doesn't "cancel out" all my lectures on reckless driving. Nothing I did was "reckless," and even if it was, I'd do anything to protect you two. That's why I came flying in on the Manticore's back to save you from that dragon. You already know how that all played out. ✳✳✳

I hope this note will end the constant questions at dinnertime. As far as I'm concerned, the subject is now closed. I did what I needed to do to for my boys to see their dad, including kicking some dragon butt and wielding a curse-crushing sword. (Remember this the next time I ask you to take out the trash. The Mighty Warrior commands you.)

Love,

Mom

THE SEARCH FOR THE PHOENIX GEM

Local New Mushroomton family and the legendary Manticore defeat creature and save town

Everybody knows how that played out!

by Sadalia brushthorn

downtown new mushroomton—A "Dragon Curse" was unleashed in downtown New Mushroomton, terrorizing residents and doing serious damage to New

Mushroomton High. One thing that is indisputable is that the city was saved by the efforts of Laurel Lightfoot and her two sons, Ian and Barley. How these ordinary citizens became involved has been the subject of

It is this Legacy. The Legacy of Zantar. Of Faldar. Of Bozark. You must strive to live up to their legends. Their contributions to the realm go far beyond the few examples cited here. Now that you know the makings of a Master Wizard, what will you do to add to this heritage? What will you leave behind? What will you gift to the next generation?

And so, Adventurer, our journey together comes to an end. But YOUR journey through the Questing Realm has just begun. There are always new Quests to seek, more characters and creatures to meet, and Magic to learn.

Yeah, those legendary wizards were all pretty cool, but nothing they gave to the next generation could compare to what Ian gave to me.

Dad and I got to say goodbye.

All my life, I wondered what it would be like to meet Dad. And then I had the chance to do so and I gave it up. Why?

It's not that I didn't want to meet him. I did, and I still do! But I realized that what I thought he would give me, what I thought I was missing, were things I already had.

Because I had Barley.

stout heart and firm frame.

Expand your knowledge and experience with these Quests of Yore Expansion Kits!

Quests of Yore: The Swamps of Despair

Quests of Yore: The Submerged City of the Mystic Merfolk

Quests of Yore: The Lost Souls of Glaive's Deep

Fare thee well, Adventurer. This chapter is over. A new one awaits....

Glossary

Ability – Skill in a particular area of interest or profession

Adventurer – A person who seeks new experiences and travels to new lands; one who is brave, bold, and unafraid of the unknown

Adversary – Someone who opposes you, your wishes, or your actions; someone who works against you

Alora the Majestic – Legendary Wizard known for her intelligence and creative Spell work; aided the citizens of Crystalwood after a devastating firestorm enveloped the town and forest

Apprentice – The lowest level of skill for a Wizard; someone who is just starting to learn the ways of Magic

Bard – A poet, singer, or other skilled storyteller who immortalizes epic tales through written or spoken word (see Fendus the Bard) (Associated terms: Fellowship; Ranger; Rogue; Warrior; Wizard)

Battle – A fight, competition, or contest between two or more adversaries

Birdar the Fanciful – Legendary Wizard known for his whimsy and imagination; had a deep connection to birds and winged creatures, which he protected for most of his life

Booby traps – Hidden danger in the form of pits, projectiles, trapdoors, and other devices intended to hinder or stop Adventurers from reaching their goal

Glossary

Bottomless Pit – Abyss or chasm that has no end; the victim, once falling, will fall forever (see Path of Peril)

Bozark the Benevolent – Legendary Wizard known for her fortitude and resilience; used her enchanted hammer to destroy the Neverending Wall to unite two warring nations

Campaign – An adventure or expedition that has a specific goal, e.g., locating a relic, helping someone in need, exploring new lands (Associated terms: Journey; Quest)

Casting magnitude – The strength, duration, concentration, and distance of a Spell

Centaur – One of the fastest species in the realm, known for their powerful legs and flowing manes

Lightfoot family!

I hope that you will all agree to be my special guests at the grand reopening of my tavern. Laurel, you already swore an oath to me in combat class, so I know you are in.

Ian and Barley, I expect you to be right there alongside your mom. It's going to be a grand and glorious party for the ages! See you there!

Love,
The Manticore

The BEAST is BACK!

The Manticore's Tavern
GRAND REOPENING

Do you have what it takes to Party with
The Manticore?

Take a risk and do it! After all,
"You have to Take Risks in Life to have an Adventure."

Join this legendary warrior for food, fun, and fire breath.
Band together! Form a Fellowship!
Join hands and hearts!

Rules will be broken!
Lines will be crossed!

THE PLACE WHERE ALL QUESTS BEGIN!

ALL ARE WELCOME!

Glossary

Journey – A trip from one place to another, usually containing the possibility of trials and adventure
(Associated terms: Campaign; Quest)

Kingsdore – One of the largest realms in the Questing Realm; known for the diversity of its inhabitants

Labyrinth – An intricate and massive maze that only the cleverest can solve (see Minotaur)

Lulling Lute – A Magical musical instrument with the power to defuse a hostile situation

Mage – The intermediate level of skill for a Wizard; someone who has some knowledge of the ways of Magic and Quests, but has not mastered the advanced Spells

Magic Decree – An additional rule for Spellcasting that a Wizard must follow in order to perform a Spell successfully

Magic Gift – A quality that is intrinsic to a character who can perform Magic

Manticore – Legendary warrior who is part lion, part scorpion, and part bat; owner of the Manticore's Tavern and her famous sword, the Curse Crusher

Manticore's Tavern – The place where all Quests begin, owned by the legendary Manticore

Master Wizard – The advanced level of skill for a Wizard; someone who has mastered the advanced Spells

Glossary

Merfolk - Creatures of the sea; have powerful tails and can withstand turbulent waters

Minotaur - The fearsome guardian of the Labyrinth

Monk - A character whose skills center on knowledge, study, and contemplation

Moonset - A remote island where the moon is known to be at its brightest and most potent

Neverending Wall - A w[...] Westphalia and Northwest [...]

Path of Peril - An expan[...] essential destination for all [...]

Phoenix - A legendary win[...] has lived a long life and is [...]

Phoenix Gem - A potent [...] and effectiveness of the mo[...]

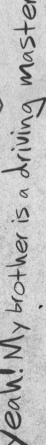

Yeah! My brother is a driving master!

The first month after the dragon battle
was pretty crazy and strange.
But things are finally settling down.

I rebuilt the school using magic.
It took a lot of work and research to figure
out which spells would be the most useful,
but Barley's endless knowledge helped a lot.

Oh, and there was one other development....

NMDMV

New Mushroomton Department of Motor Vehicles

Provisional Driver License

CLASS: C

NAME: Jandore Lightfoot **SEX:** M **SPECIES:** ELF
HT: 5'8" **HAIR:** BLUE **WT:** 141 lbs **EYES:** BROWN

ADDRESS:
313 Pennybun Lane
New Mushroomton,
United Realms

THE CITY OF NEW MUSHROOMTON · est. the Third Age

Glossary

Ranger – An explorer who traverses different realms; excellent at tracking and navigating even the most challenging terrains (Associated terms: Fellowship; Rogue; Warrior; Wizard)

Relic – An ancient object that holds a form of power or significance

Rogue – A person who is skilled at finding and obtaining objects; makes for an excellent spy on covert Quests (Associated terms: Fellowship; Ranger; Warrior; Wizard)

Satyr – A creature with a close connection to nature; also referred as the Keeper of the Forest

Shamblefoot the Wondrous – A famous Wizard who was known for his eccentricity and musical abilities; teacher of Zantar the Great

Shield of Zadar – A relic owned by the Cyclops Zadar that was used to stop the Torrential Tide from flooding the Thirteenth Colony of Desolation Island

Sprite – A small flying creature known for its friendliness and whimsy

Sprite's Lantern – An enchanted accessory that has the power to reverse Invisibility Spells and decipher coded messages

Staff – A wooden instrument that harnesses a Wizard's Magic Gift and allows them to perform Magic

Summit – The highest point, either literally or figuratively; a place where all is visible, where you can see things clearly

Tavern – A place of gathering where food, drink, and various diversions are on offer to the weary Adventurer and his or her band of comrades; a place of merriment (See Manticore's Tavern)

Speaking of driving, these are some of my ideas for Guinevere the Second.

I wanted to include a lifelike mane and flowing tail, but now I'm wondering if it's not practical.

SPARE **SPARE** TIRE

Gotta get another pegasus on the side, too!

LANCE

Should I add a Sprite-proof windshield?

SHIELD

Add more seats for the rest of the fellowship?

Maybe you don't have to worry about being practical.
A little magic can go a long way....

Sir Iandore
speaks the TRUTH!

Just think of all the quests we can pursue now!
So many possibilities . . .

Secluded Island

7

Classic Location
— Level Seven —
Start a new path on your quest. Roll for Danger & Luck.

Chamber of Doom

18

Legendary Location
— Level Eighteen —
Start a new path on your quest. Roll for Danger & Luck.

Misty Swamp

10

Classic Location
— Level Ten —
Start a new path on your quest. Roll for Danger & Luck.

Guinevere the Second is off the drawing board and on the road!

The only thing left to do was to give her a sweet paint job, but Ian already took care of it! **I LOVE IT!!**

I knew it would be tough to capture the majesty of the original Guinevere, but I thought this painting of us might do the trick!

Taking care of Guinevere the Second's paint job was the least I could do.

Without Barley, we would never have gone on the quest for the Phoenix Gem.

Thanks to Barley and this adventure, everything changed. They made me a better, happier, and BOLDER person. Made the realm a better place. A more MAGICAL place.

You should join me on another awesome quest, Master Wizard!

I hear tell of an enchanted woodland full of joy and mystery.

You mean the park? AYE!

Saddle up
Guinevere the
Second!

It's time to take the Road of Ruin.

On a quest, the clear path is never the right one.
I'm thinking Guinevere the Second
can take to the skies!

Oooh,
       sounds risky. I love it!

What's a little questing without risks?
Now, let's go. Adventure awaits....

ONWARD!

Barley   Ian

Barley

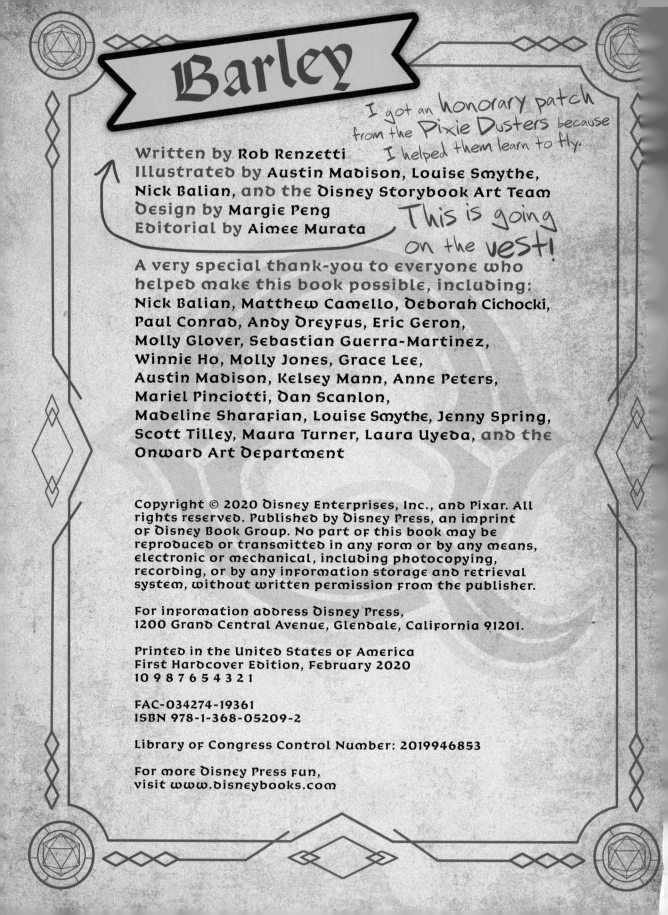

I got an honorary patch from the Pixie Dusters because I helped them learn to fly.

Written by Rob Renzetti
Illustrated by Austin Madison, Louise Smythe,
Nick Balian, and the Disney Storybook Art Team
Design by Margie Peng
Editorial by Aimee Murata

This is going on the vest!

A very special thank-you to everyone who helped make this book possible, including:
Nick Balian, Matthew Camello, Deborah Cichocki,
Paul Conrad, Andy Dreyfus, Eric Geron,
Molly Glover, Sebastian Guerra-Martinez,
Winnie Ho, Molly Jones, Grace Lee,
Austin Madison, Kelsey Mann, Anne Peters,
Mariel Pinciotti, Dan Scanlon,
Madeline Sharafian, Louise Smythe, Jenny Spring,
Scott Tilley, Maura Turner, Laura Uyeda, and the
Onward Art Department

For information address Disney Press,
1200 Grand Central Avenue, Glendale, California 91201.

Printed in the United States of America
First Hardcover Edition, February 2020
10 9 8 7 6 5 4 3 2 1

FAC-034274-19361
ISBN 978-1-368-05209-2

Library of Congress Control Number: 2019946853

For more Disney Press fun,
visit www.disneybooks.com

"SWORD OF ETERNAL BURNINESS"
+2 AGAINST FROST GIANTS

THE 7th VOYAGERS